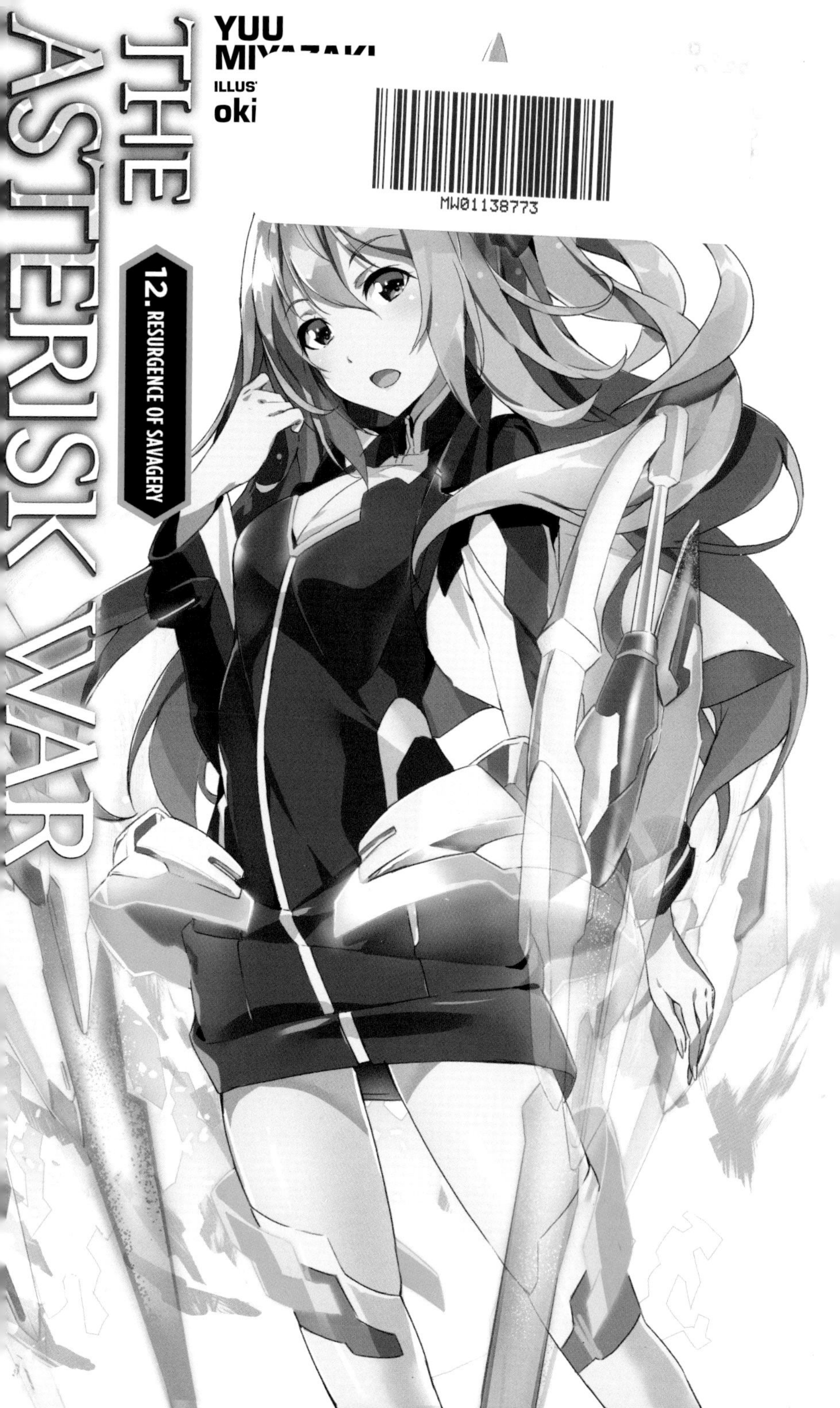
THE ASTERISK WAR
YUU
oki
12. RESURGENCE OF SAVAGERY
MW01138773

Akari Yachigusa
Akari Yachigusa
"OH...
YOU..."

"AH..."
Madiath Mesa
Madiath Mesa

Ayato Amagiri
Ayato Amagiri
"I WOULDN'T WANT YOU TO."

"I'M NOT GOING TO HOLD BACK.
THERE WOULD BE NO POINT
TO THIS IF I DID."
Haruka Amagiri
Haruka Amagiri

Saya Sasamiya
Saya Sasamiya
Julis-Alexia von Riessfeld
Julis-Alexia
von Riessfeld
Claudia Enfield
Claudia Enfield

Kirin Toudou
Kirin Toudou

THE ASTERISK WAR

12. RESURGENCE OF SAVAGERY

YUU MIYAZAKI

ILLUSTRATION: OKIURA

NEW YORK

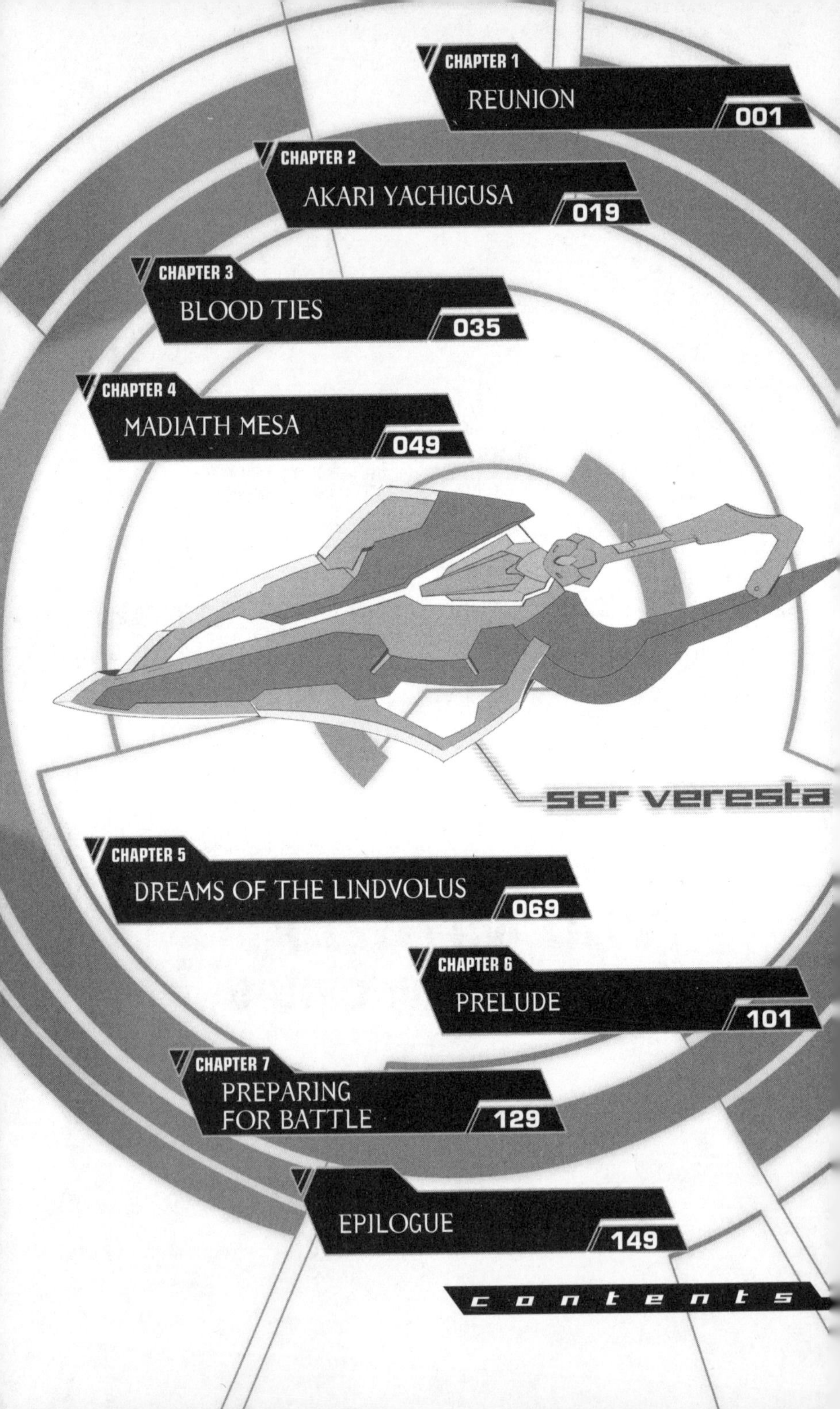

contents

SEIDOUKAN ACADEMY

AYATO AMAGIRI

The protagonist of this work. Wielder of the Ser Veresta.

ALIAS: Gathering Clouds, Murakumo
ORGA LUX: Ser Veresta

JULIS-ALEXIA VON RIESSFELD

Princess of Lieseltania. Ayato's partner for the Phoenix.

ALIAS: the Witch of the Resplendent Flames, Glühen Rose
LUX: Aspera Spina

CLAUDIA ENFIELD

Student council president at Seidoukan Academy. Leader of Team Enfield.

ALIAS: the Commander of a Thousand Visions, Parca Morta
ORGA LUX: Pan-Dora

SAYA SASAMIYA

Ayato's childhood friend. An expert in weaponry and machines.

ALIAS: none yet given
LUX: type 38 Lux grenade launcher Helnekraum, type 34 wave cannon Ark Van Ders Improved Model, and others

KIRIN TOUDOU

Disciple of the Toudou School of swordsmanship with natural talent. Saya's partner for the Phoenix.

ALIAS: the Keen-Edged Tempest, Shippuu Jinrai
LUX: none (wields the katana Senbakiri)

EISHIROU YABUKI

Ayato's roommate. Member of the newspaper club.

LESTER MACPHAIL

Number nine at Seidoukan Academy. Brusque and straightforward but has a deep sense of duty.

RANDY HOOKE

Lester's partner for the Phoenix.

KYOUKO YATSUZAKI

Ayato and company's homeroom teacher.

PREVIOUSLY IN *THE ASTERISK WAR*...

The various members of Team Enfield go their separate ways as they begin their respective preparations for the Lindvolus, with Julis training at Xinglou Fan's private school, the Liangshan; Saya taking charge of her own Lux development facility; and Claudia opening negotiations with Galaxy and meeting face-to-face with Ladislav Bartošik. Ayato and Kirin, both originally intending to go home for the New Year, find themselves paying visits to each other's families. With her help, Ayato is finally able to bring himself to face his father and requests the assistance of Magnum Opus, Hilda Jane Rowlands, to rouse his sister. At long last, Haruka awakens from her long sleep...

haracters

THE ASTERISK WAR, Vol. 12
YUU MIYAZAKI

Translation by Haydn Trowell
Cover art by okiura

Yen On
150 West 30th Street, 19th Floor
New York, NY 10001

Visit us at yenpress.com
facebook.com/yenpress
twitter.com/yenpress
yenpress.tumblr.com
instagram.com/yenpress

First Yen On Edition: January 2020

Yen On is an imprint of Yen Press, LLC.
The Yen On name and logo are trademarks of Yen Press, LLC.

The publisher is not responsible for websites (or their content) that are not owned by the publisher.

Library of Congress Cataloging-in-Publication Data
Names: Miyazaki, Yuu, author. | Tanaka, Melissa, translator. |
Trowell, Haydn, translator.
Title: The asterisk war / Yuu Miyazaki ; translation by Melissa Tanaka.
Other titles: Gakusen toshi asterisk. English
Description: First Yen On edition. | New York, NY : Yen On, 2016– |
v. 6–8 translation by Haydn Trowell | Audience: Ages 13 & up.
Identifiers: LCCN 2016023755 | ISBN 9780316315272 (v. 1 : paperback) |
ISBN 9780316398589 (v. 2 : paperback) | ISBN 9780316398602 (v. 3 : paperback) |
ISBN 9780316398626 (v. 4 : paperback) | ISBN 9780316398657 (v. 5 : paperback) |
ISBN 9780316398671 (v. 6 : paperback) | ISBN 9780316398695 (v. 7 : paperback) |
ISBN 9780316398718 (v. 8 : paperback) | ISBN 9781975302801 (v. 9 : paperback) |
ISBN 9781975329358 (v. 10 : paperback) | ISBN 9781975303518 (v. 11 : paperback) |
ISBN 9781975304317 (v. 12 : paperback)
Subjects: CYAC: Science fiction. | BISAC: FICTION / Science Fiction / Adventure.
Classification: LCC PZ7.1.M635 As 2016 | DDC [Fic]—dc23
LC record available at https://lccn.loc.gov/2016023755

ISBNs: 978-1-9753-0431-7 (paperback)
978-1-9753-0432-4 (ebook)

1 3 5 7 9 10 8 6 4 2

LSC-C

Printed in the United States of America

CHAPTER 1
REUNION

As they made their way through the subterranean depths of Asterisk's central district hospital, Julis, walking at Ayato's right-hand side, patted him on the back.

"What's the matter?" she said as she looked up at his face, her lips curling impishly. "It's not like you to be this nervous."

"R-really…?" he stammered in surprise.

"She's right. Your whole body has gone stiff." This time, it was Saya, at his left, who suddenly gave him a reassuring pat—on the butt.

"Wha—?! S-Saya?!"

"You're going to make Haru worry if you don't calm down." Despite her teasing, her voice and eyes radiated a smiling warmth.

"Come now, you two," Claudia chided. "Ayato hasn't spoken to his sister in years. Anyone would feel uneasy in his situation."

"B-but is this really okay…?" Kirin muttered. "I mean, won't we all just get in the way? After all, it's such an important moment for you…"

Ayato glanced over his shoulder at the two girls walking behind him. Their expressions were practically polar opposites: Claudia wore the same composed smile as ever, while Kirin's uneasy frown was even more pronounced than usual.

The hospital's underground medical facilities were accessible only to those who had been granted express authorization, so Ayato had asked the institute's director, Jan Korbel, to allow Julis and the others to accompany him.

"It's fine," he responded. "I've been wanting to introduce you all properly for a while now."

Ahead of them, two young, uniformed Stjarnagarm officers stood at attention at either side of the door at the end of the corridor. As was to be expected of the two women who had been handpicked by Commander Helga Lindwall, their demeanor and diligence were impeccable. Not only that, but it took only one glimpse at their confident figures to see how strong they both were.

"...Hmm, the security looks tight enough," Julis said, evidently thinking the same thing.

Ayato merely nodded in agreement.

Five days had passed since Hilda Jane Rowlands, alias Magnum Opus, had used her mana accelerator in Geneva, Switzerland, to successfully dispel the seal that had imprisoned Haruka within her own body. Through a live video feed, both Ayato and Julis had seen Haruka briefly open her eyes, but she had soon slipped back into unconsciousness. According to Hilda's medical staff, however, this time, she was merely suffering the effects of depleted prana. In other words, the procedure had gone smoothly.

As such, they had decided to bring her back to Asterisk, but as soon as they arrived at the floating airport that served the city, Helga and an assignment of security personnel were already waiting for them. While Ayato was at first taken aback by the unexpected welcoming party, Helga quickly informed him that Haruka was an important witness in her investigation into the Eclipse, and so would be guarded with the utmost caution.

Then, last night, Director Jan Korbel had contacted Ayato to let him know she had finally woken up.

And that brought them to now:

"Uhh, well," Ayato began, "I'd like to see my sister..."

"Please wait a moment." One of the guards, her expression unchanging, opened an air-window that linked into the hospital room. "Go ahead," she finally responded as she and her companion made room for them to enter.

Ayato sucked in a breath before opening the door.

The walls and floor were pure white in color. The room wasn't particularly large, and apart from the bed lying next to the wall, there was little that might have grabbed one's attention.

Even if there was, however, Ayato would have been unlikely to notice it.

His gaze was drawn immediately to his sister, sitting up in the bed—to that beaming smile that he hadn't seen in almost seven years.

"Nice to see you, Ayato."

Ayato's mouth opened reflexively at the sound of that dear voice, but no words came out. His lips trembled for a brief moment before he took a deep breath and broke out into a weak smile. "Long time no see, sis."

Haruka, dressed in a pale blue hospital gown, really hadn't changed at all from how he remembered her.

"Oh? It doesn't feel like it's been all that long to me, though…?"

Given that she had spent these last seven years asleep (or, more precisely, divorced from the flow of time), it made sense that the past wouldn't feel so distant to her.

"But even so, look how big you've gotten! I'm most surprised by that, to be honest."

"Ah, yeah…"

Even though everything might have stopped for her during that time, including her own growth, Ayato had still continued to age. Indeed, if she were still essentially the same age she had been before sealing herself away, then it was now Ayato who was the older of the two.

"But you still knew it was me, right?"

"What? Of course I did. I'm your big sis, after all!" Haruka puffed out her cheeks at the very suggestion—and then, all of a sudden, began to step down from the bed.

Ayato rushed to help her. "H-hold on, Haru! You've only just woken up…!"

"I'm fine, I'm fine. Do I really look that weak to you?"

Indeed, it turned out that her footing was solid. Normally, anyone who had been bedridden for as long as she had would wake to find their body frail beyond imagination. However, given that her sleep had been abnormal, her ability had frozen everything about herself, so that upon waking, she was just as she had been before.

"Oh? So you've finally overtaken me, huh?" Haruka said, tilting her head slightly upward as she stood before him.

This was, of course, a first for Ayato, too—never before had he been the taller of the two.

"Ah, right…! Haru, these are yours…" He took a glasses case out of his pocket, handing it to her. The glasses inside were nondescript, with somewhat rounded lenses and a black frame. He had been holding onto them ever since Saya had found them at the abandoned site of the Eclipse.

The lenses had been broken and the frame bent out of shape, but Ayato had them repaired so he could return them to their owner when the time came.

"Wow, thanks! I can't get used to a borrowed pair," Haruka exclaimed, swapping the glasses she had been wearing until now with her own. "Yep, there's no beating one's own tried-and-true!"

Indeed, her own glasses suited her the best.

"Hey, Ayato. Come a bit closer." She flashed him a gentle smile as she reached out to touch his cheek.

"Haru…?"

"…I've heard all about it. About what you've done for me, about how hard you've been fighting all this time. Thank you, Ayato."

Her words echoed in his ears, carving their way into his heart.

At the same time, he came to a sudden realization: No matter how much taller he might grow, no matter what heights he might bring his swordsmanship to, he would never be a match for her.

To him, Haruka was that great a person.

"So…are you going to introduce your friends to me, or what?"

"Ah!" Ayato turned around, only to see his four companions smiling at them somewhat nervously.

The first to speak was Saya, standing to the left. "You look good, Haru," she said, giving her a thumbs-up.

"Thanks to you. Just look how beautiful you've become, Saya!" Haruka said with a wink as she, too, flashed her a thumbs-up in turn. "Yep, I knew you had a sharper eye than Ayato..."

Saya nodded in satisfaction before turning toward him balefully. "When *he* saw me again for the first time in so long, all he said was that I hadn't changed at all."

It seemed that she still held a grudge over his remarks from almost two years ago.

"Ah, I'm—"

"Julis, right? Ayato's tag partner in the Phoenix, a princess of Lieseltania, and a beautiful, flame-wielding Strega, right? You must have such a pure heart. Thank you. I'm sure Ayato owes you a lot, too."

"Huh? N-no, I'm only..." Julis could only stare back at her, mouth agape, before lowering her head.

"And you're Claudia, the team's representative in the Gryps, right? Plus, Seidoukan's student council president, and the one who invited Ayato here on a special scholarship. And you've got the Pan-Dora, too, right? That's a pretty terrifying Orga Lux..."

"Oh dear, my fame precedes me," Claudia replied, raising a hand to her cheek before giving Haruka a light bow.

"And you're the Toudou girl, Kirin. You look so young, but I've heard that you're one of the best swordswomen in all of Asterisk. I know a thing or two myself about dueling. Won't you have a little bout with me one day?"

"Wh-wh-what...?! I—I'd be honored...!" Turning scarlet, Kirin made a deep, formal bow.

"Ah, I shouldn't keep you all standing, not when you've come to see me like this. Come here, sit, sit," Haruka said, fiddling with an air-window by her bed, when a long sofa suddenly emerged from the floor.

"...It looks like you already know everyone better than I could introduce them," Ayato remarked as he took the closest position on the sofa.

"Eh-heh, I told you, right? I've heard aaall about it. All kinds of things!" Haruka teased as she returned to her bed. "Anyway, is one of our guests your girlfriend, maybe? As your sister, I'd like to greet her properly."

"Wha—?!"

Haruka had spoken lightly, but Ayato and the four guests all turned stiff in consternation.

Haruka watched their reactions with puzzlement for a brief moment before raising a hand to her mouth, as if to take back her words. "Ah…! Sorry, I just thought… I guess I said too much, huh?" She looked at Ayato beseechingly, clearly wanting him to step in.

"Ah, I mean, the thing about that is…" He trailed off, unable to find the right words.

In the end, it was Claudia who came to his rescue: "We're all presently fighting to be the one, you see."

"H-hold on, Claudia!" Julis stammered, her cheeks turning red. "You can't just—"

Claudia raised a hand to stop her. "Fighting to be the one to look out for Ayato, of course."

"Ah, I see, I see." Haruka crossed her arms, nodding repeatedly as she gave him a meaningful gaze. "Way to go, Ayato. Who would have thought my little brother would be so popular? You've made me proud."

"…Come on, Haru, cut it out."

"Oh, is that a blush? But I guess you *are* right around that age now, huh?"

"Haru!" Ayato cried out, practically on the verge of tears.

"Hee-hee, sorry, sorry." Haruka flashed him an amused smile as she patted him on the hand.

"R-right." Julis cleared her throat. "Ayato looks like such a kid, talking to his sister like this."

Ayato had wanted to find some way to change the subject, but not like this. "I-is that so? I didn't notice…"

"No, Julis hit the mark," Saya interrupted. "You've always acted like a pampered kid in front of your sister."

"You did seem a bit more, um, emotional when we went to see your father…" Even Kirin was in agreement with the others.

Not only that, but:

"Don't worry about it, Ayato," Claudia said with a light chuckle. "That's just part of your charm."

"C-come on, you don't *all* need to…" Ayato was trying to find any way he could to shield himself from the spectacular linked attack, but Haruka, it seemed, could withstand it no further, bursting out into gales of laughter:

"*Pfft!* Ha-ha-ha-ha!"

"H-Haru…?"

"Ah, sorry. I'm just so relieved. I was worried what you'd do without me, but seeing these wonderful friends of yours… I'd already heard about everyone, but it's different meeting you all in person." She wiped away the tears welling in the corners of her eyes, her voice truly joyful.

"Right, about that. You said you'd already heard, but from whom…?"

"That would be me."

"!"

Ayato and his four companions all spun around as a voice rang out from behind them. Standing in the corner of the room, leaning against the far wall, was a tall woman.

"Commander Lindwall…?!"

"My apologies, I didn't mean to surprise you. I didn't want to barge in on your long-awaited reunion, you see." Helga Lindwall, commander of the city guard and widely considered one of the strongest fighters in all of Asterisk's history, gave the group an apologetic grin. She had probably been there from the very beginning.

He might have been focusing his attention on Haruka, but Ayato could hardly believe that not only he, but also every single member of the team that had conquered the Gryps, had failed to detect her presence.

Or rather, he was more embarrassed, perhaps, that she had witnessed their previous exchange.

"I've had a lot of tests today, so Helga's been accompanying me. She's also been filling me in on everything that I missed. She even showed me the Festa."

"I see… Thank you."

"What's this?" Helga said, raising a hand to quiet him. "There's no need for thanks. What kind of guard would I be if I didn't accompany her to her tests? And I thought it would be best to fill in some gaps in her information while I was at it."

"But…" A hint of suspicion infected Claudia's voice. "If you're inquiring about *that*, wouldn't all this new information get in the way?"

She had a point. Human memory could be an uncertain thing, and if Haruka was told what had happened during her long sleep, that new information could end up affecting her recollection of the past.

"That would normally be the case, yes," Helga responded. "But it doesn't necessarily hold for this situation. Someone involved in the Eclipse may have the ability to manipulate another person's thoughts, so there's every possibility that her memories would be unreliable anyway."

"…"

Ayato and Claudia exchanged brief glances. She was talking, of course, about the Varda-Vaos.

The two of them, along with Sylvia Lyyneheym, had joined forces with the integrated enterprise foundation Galaxy in pursuit of the Varda-Vaos's organization, the Golden Bough Alliance. This was, of course, highly confidential as far as Galaxy was concerned, and one of the conditions of their involvement was that they weren't to utter a word to anyone. Including—no, especially—the city guard.

Ayato certainly wanted to enlist the help of Stjarnagarm, considering it was one of the few organizations that seemed to legitimately want to get to the bottom of the Golden Bough Alliance, but there was no getting around his present situation. He, of course, had confidence in Helga's abilities and trusted her on a personal level, so he couldn't help but feel a touch of guilt at concealing what he knew.

But even so, coming forward wasn't something he could decide to do by himself.

"Manipulating memories? You mean, someone capable of mental interference was involved in the Eclipse...?" Julis, a Strega herself, was quick to put the pieces together.

"Indeed," Helga stated. "We suspect they're using an Orga Lux. They're likely associated with the man who attacked Ayato the night before the championship match at the Gryps—this Lamina Mortis who was involved in the Eclipse."

"What?!" All at once, Julis, Saya, Kirin (and Claudia, too, for appearance's sake) turned to Ayato in alarm.

"You said you were attacked, but you never made it out to sound *that* dangerous!" Julis was clearly angry—so angry, in fact, that she looked almost threatening.

"N-no, I mean, we had the match coming up, and I didn't really have time to explain everything in detail..."

Julis, Saya, and Kirin had nothing to do with this affair, and he had wanted to keep them from getting caught up in it unnecessarily. Indeed, if they knew too much, there was every possibility that their actions could draw an attempt on their lives just as Claudia's had.

"In fact, a number of the staff at this very hospital appear to have been attacked as well. And according to our investigations, the student in charge of the Gran Colosseo at the school fair is a victim, too. His memories, it seems, have been changed."

"But...I've never heard of an Orga Lux with that kind of power," Saya murmured doubtfully.

"Don't the integrated enterprise foundations have to disclose everything they know about their urm-manadite stocks...?" Kirin added.

Helga, however, shook her head. "There have always been exceptions. Although, in most cases, it's more a question of timing, as it's almost impossible to keep these things under wraps forever. They put an awful lot of effort into keeping tabs on one another, after all."

"So you're saying this doesn't have anything to do with the foundations at all?"

"At the very least, it does look that way for now. The Eclipse was run by Danilo Bertoni and his associates, working individually—albeit with the tacit consent of the foundations. We're likely dealing with the remnants of that group."

The commander was as sharp as ever. Even with no more than the limited information at her disposal, she was still managing to put the pieces together with frightening accuracy.

"Ah, my apologies. We've gone a little bit off track. Anyway, I thought the easiest way to tell whether Haruka's memories had been altered was to compare them against what we already know."

"Also, because I asked her to fill me in," Haruka, until now listening to their exchange in silence, suddenly interjected. "I wanted to know what's been happening over the past seven years… I mean, I could always look it up on the Net, but anything I find there is guaranteed to be one-sided, right? So I thought Helga could give me a more objective rundown."

"We've only got so much time, though, so it's really no more than a rough summary."

That was enough for Ayato. "…All right."

"Well, I can always ask you all for more intimate details. We've got time, right?"

At this, Ayato felt a strange warmth begin to spread through his chest.

They had all the time in the world.

That fact made him happier than he could possibly express.

Still, first things first:

"In that case…I've got some questions I want to ask you as well." Ayato set a grave gaze upon her as he broached the topic.

After all, there was something he needed to clarify before they could talk about anything else.

Haruka, for her part, seemed to have guessed what he meant, giving him a slight nod. "Yeah, there's some things I'd better tell you, too."

"…If it's something private, we can clear the room," Helga offered.

"Ah, yeah…thanks."

But no sooner had everyone stood up than Haruka shook her head. "No, it's related to your investigation, and I want the others to hear as well. If Ayato trusts them, then so do I."

Julis and the others exchanged glances before retaking their seats.

"Well, first of all...," Haruka continued as they sat, "Helga was right. It does look like my memories have been changed. There's a lot that doesn't seem to add up with what she told me."

"...Huh?"

She had admitted it so readily that Ayato couldn't help being taken aback, but this was more or less what he had expected.

"There are other areas that are just a complete blank... I don't know whether my memories have been erased or I just can't access them. Although it's probably more like they've been censored, I guess."

"So I was right..." Helga wrinkled her brow.

"Well, I guess we're lucky, in a way."

"What's that supposed to mean?" Ayato demanded.

Haruka looked up at him with a smile. "I mean, the Ser Veresta has chosen you now, right? That by itself is a kind of miracle."

"Huh? Well, I guess so... It's still letting me wield it. Although..."

The Ser Veresta had been badly damaged during the championship match of the Gryps, and he had just gotten it back the other day after having it repaired.

He had been worried that the experience might have soured the Orga Lux on him, but he felt nothing out of the ordinary when he tried it out, so at the very least, it didn't seem to have given up on him yet.

"Can I hold it? Just for a minute?"

"The Ser Veresta?" Only after Ayato had already removed it from the holder at his waist and handed it to her did he remember that she had been its previous user.

Which meant—

"I don't know whether Orga Luxes experience time the same way we do, but still...I suppose it's been a while for you, too. For me, it feels like we last fought together only yesterday." She spoke to it gently, before suddenly activating it.

Orga Luxes didn't even normally let anyone but their user lay a finger on them, yet this particularly difficult one accepted her so readily.

Perhaps this was to be expected of a former user? Ayato wondered.

A black pattern coiled around the pure-white blade. It was the same weapon he had grown so familiar with, and yet it was roughly half the size it normally took when he wielded it.

"Hmm, it's still a little big, maybe...," Haruka murmured, when it suddenly shrank down before their eyes, until it was no longer than a dagger.

"Well, that is something. Your force of will over it is splendid. But your control over your prana is even more impressive." Helga stroked her chin in admiration.

"We're all counting on you to wield it that well, too, Ayato," Claudia said with a sweet grin.

"Uh..." He had no response to that.

No matter how much he trained, he still hadn't been able to adjust the Orga Lux to an optimal size. Fine control over his prana just wasn't his strong suit.

"I know you're partnered with Ayato now, but won't you lend me a little of your power for old times' sake, Ser Veresta?" Haruka closed her eyes before spinning the dagger-sized blade across one hand, grasping it by the hilt with the other, and raising it in front of her forehead.

That was all she did, but her movements were extraordinarily beautiful.

"What perfect swordplay..." Kirin's voice was filled with wonder.

At that moment, a faint tremor passed through the Ser Veresta, and the room was bathed in crimson red.

"—!"

Ayato covered his face with his arms, but the energy wave wasn't the burning heat he had been expecting.

"...*Phew.*" Haruka let out a deep sigh as she deactivated the Orga Lux, returning it to its holder. "Thank you, Ser Veresta. I feel much better now." And with that, she handed it back to Ayato.

"Haru, don't tell me you just...?"

"Hmm? All I did was burn away the parts of my memory that had been tampered with. I did a pretty good job, I think."

She spoke so casually that Ayato didn't know whether to be impressed or appalled.

"What?!" Julis exclaimed in astonishment. It seemed she felt the same.

"...Way to go, Haru. That'll show them," Saya added, nodding.

Ayato, having wielded the Ser Veresta for close to two years now, knew just how extraordinarily difficult it could be to handle. True, it had the ability to burn through practically anything, even the abilities of Dantes and Stregas, and those of other Orga Luxes, too, for that matter—he himself had made use of that power countless times over by now—but it was bordering on insanity to turn it against oneself.

At least, it should have been.

But what she had done went far beyond his own level of skill—she had burned away only the ability that had been placed on her, leaving the rest untouched. Only someone with a true mastery of the Orga Lux's power could hope to pull off such a feat.

"Now that that's done with, where should we begin...?" she asked in her usual calm manner.

Indeed, she hadn't changed at all from how Ayato remembered her.

*

"...My manipulation has been broken," Varda suddenly announced.

Madiath and Dirk, until that moment debating with each other about how best to push forward with the plan, gazed at her.

"How do you mean?" Madiath asked.

They were in the Golden Bough Alliance's regular meeting place, aboard their airship in the skies above Asterisk.

The meeting was taking place earlier than usual, but as they had set a course away from the city, they were unlikely to attract any unwanted attention.

"The adjustments I made to Haruka Amagiri's recollections. I don't know how she did it, but she has likely regained her original memories."

Dirk's eyes snapped open in alarm. "How the hell is that power of yours so easily broken?"

"It shouldn't be possible by anyone of this world. However, I made the changes to her memory while she was in a sealed state, so it's possible the effect was incomplete. On top of that, I didn't exactly have a lot of time."

As far as Varda's mental interference ability was concerned, whether it was brainwashing or the manipulation of memories, the more time she had to complete her work, the more effective—and more reliable—the result.

Apparently, once she had taken over the body of professor Ladislav Bartošik, it had taken her almost a full year to brainwash his students sufficiently to turn them into Genestella supremacists and bring about the Jade Twilight Incident. The majority of them, though long since imprisoned, were still subject to that brainwashing and hadn't even realized for themselves what had been done to them.

"If it isn't someone of this world, then it must have been an Orga Lux. In which case, it was probably the Ser Veresta. It is in the possession of her younger brother," Madiath pointed out. "I doubt he's reached the stage where he could cut through your powers himself, but in her hands, it wouldn't come as too much of a surprise."

Dirk turned his hateful, disgusted gaze on Madiath. "Is this really the time to be so blithe? Or maybe you're finally showing your true colors?" His voice was low and dark, as if welling up from the depths of hell. When truly angry, his usual rage and indignation subsided, a deadly calm taking their place.

Madiath, however, merely leaned back in his chair, flashing him a purposefully provocative smile. "You mean to say I've been ignoring your warnings?"

"...If we had disposed of her when I said so, this would never have happened. Am I wrong?"

"Hmm." Instead of responding to the accusation, Madiath merely reached for the holder at his waist and activated the Raksha-Nada. The gigantic, crimson blade burst forth, stopping just inches from the tip of Dirk's nose.

"What's this supposed to be? Do you really think you can intimidate me?"

"Ha-ha, no. I wouldn't expect that of you."

If Dirk had been that easy to scare, he never would have been brought into the Golden Bough Alliance to begin with.

"Perhaps showing will be more effective than telling, in this case."

"What?" Dirk's dubious gaze ran down the length of the weapon—until his eyes suddenly flashed in surprise. "*Tch*... I see. So you made contingencies."

Still watching his colleague, Madiath continued: "Think of Varda's adjustments to her memory as having been little more than insurance. I told you, didn't I? We've taken all necessary precautions. Of course, we won't be able to prevent at least some information from leaking out...but anything that she does remember would only relate to the old plan. Not the current one."

"...And what about your identity?"

"My trust in her has never run that deep. What she knows isn't enough to find her way back to me."

"You're forgetting that Ayato Amagiri has that little vixen with him. If she were to use Galaxy's database..."

"There's no need to worry about that," Madiath answered. "Luckily for us, Varda has been establishing a number of associates on the inside for quite a few years now. Any hazardous information that they had has long since been taken care of."

Dirk glared back at him in silence for a long moment, as if to sound out his true intentions. Finally, he let out a brief sigh before reclining back in his sofa and putting his legs up on the table in front of them. "Fine. I'll take your word for it. For now."

"I would say the commander of the city guard poses a greater risk. If she manages to dig something up—no matter how out-of-date it might be—there's every likelihood that *she* might be able to find a connection leading back to me."

"I'll take care of that. If the city guard's got more work than they can handle, that old hag won't have any time left for old investigations."

"In that case, it wouldn't hurt to sacrifice a few pawns."

Madiath wasn't unappreciative of his two colleagues' suggestions, but he understood, even if they didn't, that anything too conspicuous could backfire on them.

"Well, if push comes to shove, we can always move the plan forward a little."

That was really the only sensible option available to them right now.

And, of course, he had Haruka Amagiri to thank for that.

Not only had she completely crushed the previous plan, she was beginning to cause them problems all over again.

And yet—

"Well then, perhaps it's time we called it a day?" With that, he rose to his feet, returning the Raksha-Nada to its holder at his waist. As he left the cabin for the narrow deck outside, a powerful blast of wind suddenly bore down on him.

Beneath him, the city of Rikka sparkled brilliantly amid the dark of night.

From his place in the sky, the scenery looked to have barely changed at all since he had first stepped foot in this city more than twenty years ago.

But, of course, changed it had.

The passage of time washed over everything—cities, people, even memory and passions.

"My apologies, Haruka, but this is the best I can do for you," he murmured under his breath. "Even if you are Akari's daughter… No, precisely *because* you're Akari's daughter, I suppose."

As Madiath Mesa reminisced, his eyes drifted shut, and he let the past slowly overtake him.

CHAPTER 2
AKARI YACHIGUSA

"Now then, that completes the formalities. Welcome to Seidoukan Academy, Madiath Mesa." A youth with glasses closed the air-window in front of him, a courteous if practiced smile rising to his lips. "We only offer special scholarships to those we have the highest hopes for."

"I'll do my best to live up to your expectations," a young man with unruly blond hair and unusually mature features—Madiath—replied with an eloquent smile.

Well...to a point, he added to himself.

They were in the student council room on the top floor of the high school building. Outside the oversized window lay an unbroken view of Rikka, the city of Asterisk, the staging area of the world-renowned Festa.

He had finally succeeded in making his way to this city.

Or rather, strictly speaking, what he had succeeded in doing was getting the city to take him away from his past.

"Come now, you survived eight years at the Vigridhr," his companion, the student council president, said, patting him on the shoulder. "Just keep doing what you're good at, and you'll be fine."

"...I hope so" was all Madiath said in response.

There were several ways of being admitted to one of Asterisk's six schools, with some ways officially sanctioned, and others not so much. In the former category, there were those who found success in one of the several tournaments that ranked below the Festa, such as the Rondo or the Shikai Tengi. Among the latter, there were those who had been cultivated by the Research Institute, a secretive organization that focused on developing the innate talents and abilities of its subjects from early childhood—and there were still others who were selected thanks to their performance in one of the many underground battle tournaments that took place throughout the world as a form of entertainment for the masses.

The Vigridhr was one such tournament, albeit a famously brutal one. Unlike many others, it utilized video distribution rather than live audiences and had a business model reliant on gambling. Like the Festa, it pitted Genestella against Genestella, although occasionally, non-Genestella armed with conventional weapons would be entered into it, too—typically cannon fodder who had been ruined by debt, or were being punished for failing one underworld boss or another. Not only was it common for entrants to be killed in the course of battle, but for many of its fans, that was one of the tournament's main drawing cards. Madiath himself had lost count of how many opponents he had killed in his eight years fighting there, but he felt not an ounce of guilt over his actions.

That was just how things were done in that world.

He was an orphan, purchased by the organizers to fight for them. His memories of his life before that, of living as little more than a street rat in some nondescript slum, were faint and distant. He couldn't even remember his parents' faces.

In order to stay out of reach of the law, the Vigridhr was conducted aboard a large airship that was continuously on the move. Madiath had spent almost half his life in the gloom-filled dungeon at the bottom of that vessel. There were always around a hundred others with whom he had shared his fate at any given time—former participants in the real Festa, captured criminals, or dropouts who had since turned to mercenary work. And there was always a small number of child fighters like himself. The Vigridhr catered to a wide variety of tastes.

Some fighters didn't even last a month before disappearing forever (and, of course, there were children among that group, too), but those who could adapt themselves to their new status in life were generally able to hold out longer, with some even lasting several years. Madiath was one such individual and, though only a child, had been able to successfully hone his abilities to ensure his own survival.

In other words, he had achieved a sort of balance.

In these kinds of underground battle tournaments, strength alone wasn't enough to live on. If you were too strong, you would be put into increasingly dangerous matches, and that would inevitably shorten your expected lifespan. In a more legitimate setting, it was perfectly reasonable to withdraw after sustaining a critical injury, but places like the Vigridhr afforded their fighters no such option.

At the same time, the weak were simply used up until they were spent, before being discarded.

As such, the trick to survival was to find a balance, to be just capable enough—to survive, but not to enter the top rankings.

Not only was Madiath exceptionally capable of maintaining that balance, he knew how to please the bookmakers to ensure his continued value. He knew instinctively when his victory would or wouldn't benefit the organizers of the tournament and didn't mind losing so long as he could do so unscathed.

In other words, amid the disposable goods that were the tournament's fighters, he had managed to increase his value to such an extent that even the organizers had a vested interest in his continued survival.

That was how he had managed to survive in that place for eight whole years—until finally, he was scouted out by Seidoukan Academy.

In spite of everything, Madiath didn't begrudge his lot in life. This world had always been a place of inequality and unfairness, the fortunes of its denizens riding almost entirely on luck. The real question was how to make use of that fact.

That was why Madiath didn't want for much. He would be happy just to live in peace and comfort, as much as was possible. He'd had his fill of life and death and wanted nothing more to do with that world. If he could make use of his talents, he was sure he could find another way.

That was his only wish.

At least, it had been then.

*

"I'll call again," Madiath said with a smile and a wave as he bade farewell to the sweet-voiced woman at his favorite establishment.

The Rotlicht was overflowing with brilliant lights in every color imaginable. He slipped into the backstreets, hoping to avoid the drunks and solicitors who lined the main road.

The air in this part of the city was stagnant, but the warm spring nights were pleasantly comfortable.

A year had passed since he had first arrived in Asterisk.

He had been living a quiet life, almost exactly as he had planned.

Having been invited to Seidoukan on a special scholarship, he was obliged to show some level of performance, so he made sure to get himself listed at number forty-four. It would certainly have been possible for him to make the Named Cult, or even the very top of the list, but he had no desire to deal with all the troubles that that would bring.

His living expenses were covered by his scholarship, and thanks to his current position, he received enough money to occasionally enjoy himself in the city's entertainment district. He had a warm room, ate three meals a day, and, every now and then, engaged in a little contest or had a bit of fun—in other words, it was his ideal lifestyle.

He did have a certain obligation to Seidoukan, however, and being enrolled on a special scholarship, he, of course, had to earn a certain amount of points for the academy in the Festa—but he could no doubt satisfy those requirements just by entering the tournament. In any event, he could worry about that later.

He had plenty of time yet until he graduated from the academy's college. And until then, he would enjoy his life to the fullest extent possible.

Those were the thoughts running through his mind as he made his way through the Rotlicht—when, all of a sudden, he was struck by a sense of danger and stopped immediately.

He peered deeper into the alleyway ahead of him out of sheer curiosity, until, in the tight space between two buildings, he could make out a group of what looked like Le Wolfe students circling a lone woman. Judging by her gaudy dress, she must have been a worker at one of the local establishments.

Unlike the woman, who was perfectly calm, the five men surrounding her looked incensed and were each brandishing Luxes of one kind or another. They also seemed to be somewhat drunk.

Even so, their quarrel seemed to be purely verbal—at least, until one of the men let out a blaring shout and rushed toward her.

However, at that moment, there was a sudden pulse of mana, and the glow of the men's Luxes was simultaneously extinguished.

The quintet, clearly panicked, threw their Luxes to the ground and flew toward her with their fists alone.

"Heh..."

The next instant, the men all lay sprawled on the ground, and Madiath found himself overcome by a sense of admiration.

Her assailants might not have been much to begin with, but even so, taking them all down at once, without even having to lift a finger, was nothing short of impressive.

After a short pause, however, the woman suddenly tottered, raising her hands to her face as she fell to her knees—though, as far as Madiath could tell, not one of her assailants had managed to land a blow on her.

He watched on suspiciously, leaning down to pick up a large stone lying on the ground.

One of the five men, his face contorted in pain, stumbled to his feet, fumbling to ready his pistol-type Lux. Its manadite core had already begun to emit a brilliant light, his finger narrowing around the trigger—when Madiath, one step ahead of him, threw the large rock straight into his face.

The man, blood gushing from his nose, fled.

Unperturbed, Madiath squatted down and held out a hand to the woman. "Are you all right, Miss?"

Judging by her appearance, she seemed to be slightly older than he was. He couldn't really say that her flashy dress suited her, but her facial features were perfectly, beautifully symmetrical. Her hair, reaching down to her waist, was a light pink in color, like the cherry blossoms that would be in bloom right around this time of year.

"...Thank you," she said as she brought her ragged breathing under control. She looked up at him with a faint smile.

"There's no need for that. I did it out of impulse."

That was the truth.

By nature, Madiath spared little thought for others. Even if other people were suffering, so long as it didn't affect him, he didn't care what happened to them.

"I guess I got involved with some bad clients. We run an honest place, unlike most of the other establishments around here, but we must have let down our guard..." The woman let out a resigned sigh.

"I see. That's unfortunate. Anyway, are you okay? With strength like yours, I doubt any of these thugs would've been able to take you down."

"Ah, um, well..." The woman, stammering, averted her gaze.

"Right. Well, take care, then."

If she didn't want to talk, he wouldn't hang around. He turned to leave, giving her a light wave, when—

"Um, please, don't go. At least let me give you something to thank you..."

So she began, but once more, the woman fell silent.

"Don't worry about it," he said over his shoulder. "But if you really want to, I guess you can buy me something to eat if we bump into each other again."

But the Rotlicht, of course, had a high turnover of both clients and

establishments. Nor, for that matter, did Madiath frequent this particular section of it. He was unlikely to ever see her again.

Or so he had thought. And yet—

"Ah..."

"Oh..."

The next day, as he arrived at the school cafeteria for lunch, he came across the pink-haired woman standing right next to the ticket machine.

"You...?!" they exclaimed in unison.

"...So you're a senior here," Madiath said, staring at her collegiate uniform.

"And you're a high schooler. You must be very mature to hang around that kind of place late at night," she said with a hint of rebuke.

"...Madiath Mesa. Second-year at the high school here."

"Akari Yachigusa. Second-year at the college here." This time, the woman—Akari—held out her hand to him.

Madiath himself didn't know exactly why, but he found himself hesitating for the briefest of moments before accepting it.

"Well, Madiath. Let me treat you to lunch, as promised," she said with a faint, evanescent smile.

*

Before they knew it, Madiath and Akari found themselves getting to know each other.

That said, Madiath was, of course, a high school student, and Akari a college student. They were generally in different parts of the campus, so they weren't able to meet all that often. Rather, they would bump into each other maybe once or twice a week in the cafeteria and sit down to talk over lunch.

"By the way, Akari, why are you working in the Rotlicht?" Madiath asked one day over a plate of tandoori chicken.

Akari responded with an amused, if somehow bitter, smile. "For money, of course."

Madiath had only come to realize it lately, but Akari often wore such a smile—or rather, it seemed as if she seldom wore any other expression.

"But why there?"

From what he understood, the place where Akari worked was no more than a drinking hole, and thereby better than most other establishments in the area. That didn't change the fact, however, that it was still the Rotlicht. Perhaps it would have sounded strange coming from him, but he doubted that any respectable student would dare go near the place.

"I need to pay for my tuition and living expenses, you see."

"Oh...?"

Tuition at Seidoukan—or any of Asterisk's six schools, for that matter—wasn't particularly expensive, but it was enough to pose problems for anyone who had to cover it themselves. All the more so if they had to pay for their own living expenses, too.

While Madiath, who was on a special scholarship, was an exception, the vast majority of students were supported by their families. There was no shortage in Asterisk of those who had been blessed in that way. He had always thought of Akari as one such person.

Still, that wasn't what he wanted to know right now.

"In that case, why not try to get ranked? You'd have no problem making it, with your abilities."

The power that he had watched her wield that day had been considerable. The way he saw it, she was in no way inferior to Seidoukan's Page Ones.

"That's... I don't want to draw attention to myself." Once more, she flashed him that smile, tinged, somehow, with a touch of sadness.

She didn't seem to want to talk about it.

"...But that goes for you too, Madiath, doesn't it?"

"Huh?"

"I saw your ranking match the other day. It looked like you were going easy on your opponent, like you weren't putting everything you had into it," Akari said as she lifted a spoonful of curry toward her mouth.

"Heh..." Madiath couldn't help but feel somewhat chagrined by her observation.

It was certainly true that he had been selected to participate in a ranking match the other day, but he was sure to put in just enough effort to meet the school's expectations of its forty-fourth-ranked fighter. He thought of it as a performance of sorts, a way for the school to show off their prized special scholarship student. He always thought of the matches that way.

"No way, you're telling me you saw through that?" He dipped his head slightly.

"I see," the young woman said in a low voice, leaning forward. "So I was right. Don't worry. I won't tell."

"Thanks," Madiath responded, staring back at her carefully.

Now, for the first time, he found himself truly interested in this Akari Yachigusa.

"...Um? What's wrong? Is there something on my face?" Akari had turned slightly pink.

"No. I was just thinking how much you must like that curry."

"It's delicious. Why don't you try some?"

"...I'll pass."

The curry was the hottest item on the cafeteria's menu by a long shot—excruciatingly so.

Even when he was just looking at it from across the table, the fragrance was enough to make his eyes burn.

Akari, who until now had been eating it without even the slightest hint of trouble, suddenly rested her spoon beside the plate. "By the way, Madiath. There's something I've been wanting to ask you."

"Yeah?"

"...Have you ever heard of anything called the Eclipse?"

"'The Eclipse'...? I don't think so."

She certainly didn't seem to be referring to the astronomical phenomenon.

"Why do you ask?"

"No, it's okay. Forget I said anything." She flashed him another smile before going back to her curry.

"…" Madiath merely stared at her in silence for a long moment.

He had long suspected she was hiding something deeper, something she wouldn't volunteer no matter how he asked her, but he guessed this was something different yet again.

But that wasn't what was bothering him. Rather, it was her sheer evasiveness. He found it so tedious.

In which case…

Still watching her, he said, with a somewhat artificial smile: "Why don't we go on a date?"

"…Huh?" The spoon fell from her hand with a light clatter. She remained frozen in place for a drawn-out breath as she turned scarlet all the way to the tips of her ears.

It was an awfully pure response for someone who worked in the Rotlicht.

"Um… You're joking, right?"

"Nope, I'm serious."

"But I've got classes this afternoon…"

"It's okay to skip them once in a while."

At this, her eyes began to dart to and fro. "Surely, it won't be any fun…for you, I mean…with me. I'm not—"

"I don't know about that… I, for one, think it'd be plenty fun."

"But I mean, there's so many places, I don't know if I can afford to—"

"Since I invited you, I'll pay."

"No, I couldn't ask that of a high schooler—"

"Well, then we'll just have to go somewhere that doesn't cost anything." Madiath, unwilling to take no for an answer, shone her a satisfied smile.

"Ahhh…" After she sighed, once more, that somehow bitter smile rose to Akari's lips. "I see… A date it is, I guess."

He might have called it a date, but Madiath didn't really have anything special planned.

They simply strolled through the commercial area, window-shopping as they discussed all manner of trifling topics.

However, when they stopped at a small park on the edge of the residential area to take a break, Akari seemed to be in good spirits.

"...It's nice here," she whispered as the wind brushed through her rose-colored hair.

There was nothing particularly special about the park other than the fact that it met the water's edge. It didn't have any children's play equipment, but from atop the small hill covered in grass, it was possible to see as far as the other side of the crater lake. The sun was beginning to make its descent, the heavens tinged with color.

"Ah, the sky looks so wide from down here," Madiath said as he lay down on the grass, staring up at the indigo expanse.

"The sky...?" Akari tilted her head toward him.

Madiath tapped the ground at his side, urging her to join him.

As she timidly lay down beside him, she let out a sigh of contentment. "I see what you mean... This is actually pretty relaxing."

"Right? You know, where I used to live, I wasn't able to see the sky for such a long time. So it's refreshing, being able to stare at it like this now."

To Madiath, who had spent his childhood in the hull of a cramped, gloomy airship, that high, expansive sky was a symbol of freedom.

"...Really?"

"You've heard of the Vigridhr, right? That's where I come from. I can't imagine anything worse than that filthy, reeking place. But I guess I wasn't particularly aware of the sky back then. I only realized how good it feels to be absorbed into it after I got out."

Of course, Asterisk, too, was its own kind of prison.

But even so, the fact that he was able to have hope for the future, the fact that the world was now filled with color, meant that it was a completely different one.

"...Yes, I understand. It's the kind of thing you only realize after you've seized freedom." There was a strong sense of feeling to those words—something other than sympathy. "For a caged bird, the cage is the whole world," she murmured, before falling silent, still staring up at the sky.

The evening glow was soon swallowed by darkness. As the lights around the park came on, she began to speak: "I'm…an unwanted child."

Her voice was stripped clean of both sadness and anger, but beneath that vaguely bitter smile that rose to her lips, Madiath detected hollowness and a sense of loss.

"My family's worn the Yachigusa name for centuries, as a badge of honor. But then I was born, a Genestella. Unwanted, shunned by everyone around me. Even my own mother…"

Madiath said nothing, merely listening in silence.

"Even in my earliest memories, I lived alone, in a tiny little building cut off from everyone else. Whenever I saw the sky outside, everything felt so cramped, so small… Ah, um, sorry. I guess I'm getting carried away, talking about this…" Akari stumbled over her words as she came away from the reverie of the sky.

She may have had a difficult upbringing, but Madiath spared no pity for her. The world was filled with unfairness, with cruelty, with suffering.

But there *was* something, something bordering on sympathy, that brushed faintly against the inside of his chest.

"Even though you're the one who started us down this conversation…"

"Yeah," Madiath answered, his lips curling in a teasing smile. "You don't have many friends, do you?"

"…You can be pretty mean, huh." Akari, still wearing her own meaningful smile, pouted.

"Ha-ha, did you think I was some kind of saint?"

"Well… It's true there aren't a lot of people I would call friends. Only one, I suppose. She's already been married off, so we don't get to talk very often…" She stared off into the distance longingly.

"Huh. Looks like we've got more in common than I thought," Madiath answered with a chuckle.

"I thought you were pretty popular, though?" Akari asked, her voice filled now with surprise.

"I can socialize, sure. But only because I have to. I wouldn't call those people friends."

"I see… I guess you're right." She nodded in reluctant agreement.

"Well, it's getting cold. We should head back." Madiath rose to his feet, brushed off his trousers, and held out a hand to her.

"Thank you," she said as he helped her up.

Even after she had risen to her feet, however, Madiath still didn't let go. "Now then," he began. "What exactly is this Eclipse you mentioned?"

Akari, surprised, tried to pull away, but Madiath held firm.

"I'd like to know more."

"It isn't… I mean…"

"It can't be as serious as what we were just talking about, right?"

She hesitated for a moment until, perhaps convinced by this logic, she began: "I don't know much about it myself. That's why I asked you. Just in case you did… All I know is that it's some kind of fighting tournament."

"Hmm… And?" Madiath showed no sign of moving, nor of letting her go.

"…One of the customers at the shop suggested I sign up to it," she continued reluctantly. "He'd heard what I'd done to those guys from Le Wolfe the other day. He said if I had the skill and needed the money, it would be worth my while. It sounds like you can earn a lot in just one night there. But he told me to keep quiet about it…"

"That sounds pretty shady."

"…Right?" Akari responded with a sigh.

"Do you need it that much? The money?"

"The truth is… The city guard has cracked down on the shop, and we've had to stop doing business for a while. So it's been hard."

"I see."

That was enough for Madiath to get a grasp of the situation.

This Eclipse sounded like the kind of thing he had been forced to fight for in his past life. He had never suspected that something similar could be taking place right under the nose of the world's most popular legitimate battle tournament.

"So are you planning to do it?"

"...To be honest, I'm thinking about it. At this rate, it's only a matter of time until I'm kicked out of school."

No matter the reason, the integrated enterprise foundations didn't forgive those who failed to pay their tuition. The story might have been different if she had demonstrated some other form of value to them, but an unranked student like her would be expelled without even a second thought.

"...I don't want to leave just yet," she said, her gaze downcast. The hand gripping his was filled with an unexpected strength.

"In that case..."

Madiath himself was surprised by the words that rose to his lips.

What he wanted most was a life of peace and comfort. That was why he had come to Asterisk. And now he was about to poke his head into something that was clearly the polar opposite of what he had worked so hard to achieve.

And yet, despite all that—

"I'll join you, then," he declared. "Maybe I can do something to help."

CHAPTER 3
BLOOD TIES

"Well then, where should we begin...?" Haruka asked, her chin cupped in her hand, as if sorting through her newly recovered memories.

Ayato, having returned the Ser Veresta to its sheath at his waist, made himself comfortable in his seat before spinning around to look at her.

"Ah, but before we get to that, there's something I'd like to ask... Ayato. Did Dad tell you about my birth?"

"Yes," he replied, nodding. "It was just the other day, though, actually."

"I see..." At this, Haruka turned downward, her gaze vaguely forlorn.

"But nothing's changed between us, at least as far as I'm concerned. I mean, I was surprised, of course, but that was all."

That was the honest truth.

Sure, the knowledge had come as a shock, but Haruka was still his sister.

"...Thank you, Ayato." She smiled, until—

"—!"

—she gasped, gripping her chest.

Ayato rushed to put a hand on her shoulder. "Haruka...!"

But before he could reach her, she raised her own hand in an attempt to reassure him. "Sorry. I'm okay. Don't worry," she said with a forced smile.

"...That might be asking too much. Are you really okay?"

Despite her protests, he couldn't help worrying given her present condition.

"Yep. Really, really. It's just a headache. I mean, Dr. Korbel said I was fine, right? So there's no problem."

"Well...if you say so..."

If that was the opinion of the best doctor in the city, then he had little ground to argue.

"But if you do feel unwell, make sure you tell someone right away."

"Got it." Haruka nodded before taking a deep breath and staring at him seriously. "All right... Well, I got a letter one hot summer day, from someone claiming to be my real father."

"...Your real father?" Julis murmured in surprise.

Saya nudged her with her foot. "*Shh*," she warned, a finger raised to her lips.

Julis said nothing more, a look of chagrin falling over her as she returned to her seat.

"A woman who said she worked for him gave it to me on my way back from school," Haruka continued. "It... He'd written about Mom—things that I never knew about her. And he invited me to meet him."

As she spoke, Ayato realized that this was the first time he had ever seen her this way—her voice cool and detached, devoid of any trace of emotion.

"Of course, I didn't want to believe it at first or have anything to do with him. But then, it was true that I didn't really know much about Mom. So I looked into things a bit myself, but there didn't seem to be anything that really contradicted what he'd said in that letter..."

"What exactly did he say?" Ayato asked, bracing himself for her response.

Haruka, however, merely shook her head. "There weren't a lot of details, unfortunately. Only that she'd thrown everything away and started a new life somewhere else."

"She ran away...?"

At this, Haruka leaned closer to him, her gaze boring deep into his eyes. "Yes. Her face, her name, her identity—she threw it all away to become someone else. That's what he wrote."

"Wha—?!"

Ayato, it seemed, wasn't the only one taken aback by this revelation.

Julis, Saya, and Kirin, having followed along in silence until now, were visibly shocked.

"B-but that isn't—"

"Oh, it's possible," Claudia interrupted. "For the IEFs, that is. Of course, it would be a lot of work, turning a person into someone else. There's all the data to think about as well. It isn't the kind of thing they would be willing to attempt without adequate justification—that is, unless there was some kind of profit to be made, or else..."

"Or else they were granting a wish from the Festa," Julis finished for her.

"But in that case, shouldn't we just check the past winners...?" Kirin asked, her voice muted. "If we look over all of them..."

"It won't be that easy." This time, it was Helga's turn to speak. "The number of winners who keep their wishes secret is by no means inconsiderable. It is also possible someone else might have requested it on her behalf."

"I see..."

As it happened, Ayato, too, had used his wish to help someone else—to have Hilda Jane Rowlands's penalty revoked in exchange for her aid in waking Haruka.

On top of that, Ernest Fairclough had once told him that students at Gallardworth often used their wishes to prove their worth by benefiting those around them.

That being the case, they couldn't discount the possibility that Ayato's and Haruka's mother had relied on someone else's assistance. And if that was the case, then finding out who she had been would be all the more difficult.

"There is a chance, if the wish was made to Galaxy—that is, if your mother was a student at Seidoukan—that there might be some data that I can dig up... Although I suspect that any such data may have been altered, just as it was on the Ser Veresta. If she was a student at one of the other schools, then I'm afraid I'm out of ideas. The Festa Executive Committee ought to keep records of everything, but I doubt they would grant Galaxy access to any of it. On top of that, the other foundations would oppose us right from the start. More importantly, however, if the wish was to have her past erased, I doubt that even those records would have survived."

Ayato could find no fault in Claudia's reasoning.

"Well, putting that question aside… I wanted to find out the truth, so I agreed to meet him. There was a chance that whoever wrote it could be my father after all," Haruka said, returning to her account. "Around a week after I received that letter, the woman who had given it to me came back for my response… She took me to a black car where this guy with a weird, creepy mask was waiting."

"A mask…?!" Ayato blurted out, suddenly freezing in place.

"…He was the one who claimed to be my father. He called himself Lamina Mortis."

A bolt, the likes of which Ayato had never before experienced, coursed down his body.

Him…! He's *Haruka's father?!*

"I see," Helga said with a nod, her fists clenched. "So that's the connection." Her voice was so low that it was almost inaudible.

"I could tell right away that the man—Lamina Mortis—was dangerous. And strong. He was polite, and his voice was calm, but that was obviously just a facade. No one would be able to fully conceal the level of hatred that burned inside him." Haruka's words were tinted with a vague sense of frustration.

According to Dirk Eberwein, Haruka had been defeated by Lamina Mortis during the Eclipse. Ayato, too, had crossed swords with the man and didn't doubt for a second the depths of his power or his capacity to bear a grudge against the world.

"He looked me over, as if he was sizing me up. And then he asked me to help him carry out his plan."

"His plan…?"

"Yes. An unbelievably delusional, destructive plan," Haruka said with a deepening frown.

*

"I don't know how to respond, hearing this all of a sudden," Haruka said to the masked man sitting across from her.

That man—Lamina Mortis—seemed to glare back at her. "Not even if it's a request from your father?" he asked with a regretful sigh.

With only Haruka and Lamina Mortis present, the spacious interior of the limousine felt unoccupied, its leather seats uncomfortably empty. The air-conditioning was so strong that she couldn't help feeling as if she had entered a world apart from the blistering heat outside.

"You can't expect me to go along with what you're saying when you won't even show me your face or tell me your name. And I haven't accepted you as my father yet."

"Whether you accept it or not, it's an objective fact. Speaking for myself, that's enough for me. What could be more important than having our daughter see the plan through at my side?" Lamina Mortis declared with a puckered grin. "I will, of course, reveal everything once it's finished—my face, my name, and your mother, too."

"...I'm not interested. Excuse me."

She knew now that she shouldn't have come here.

But as she rose to her feet, Lamina Mortis called out to hold her back: "Haven't you heard? Your mother is dead. Murdered, as it were."

"...What?" At this, Haruka turned back toward him, her ire piqued. "Don't lie. My mom was sick—"

"That would be Sakura Amagiri, no? That carcass of hers isn't what I'm talking about. No, I mean your mother as she was before her death."

"!" Almost reflexively, Haruka swung her right arm upward, but before she could strike, the man caught her by the wrist.

"...She was murdered. I can't forgive that. That's all," he said, his masked gaze staring deep into her soul.

There was no hint of insanity in those eyes, yet there was no hatred, either. It had resembled that at first, but it was something else—a deep emptiness that somehow surpassed hatred.

After what seemed like an eternity, he pushed her away, returning to his seat. "I may have asked you to lend me your power, but don't think for a moment that I need it. The plan is already entering its final stages. I'll be satisfied just to have you at my side. Although there's no denying that ability of yours would make for good protection…

"In any event, I've already gotten you enrolled at Seidoukan. You can wait there until the final preparations are complete."

Haruka felt her temper flaring hotter with each passing sentence. "How dare you…!"

"Yes, you have a younger brother, don't you?"

"—!" Haruka caught her breath at the sudden change.

"Well, I can't say I'm particularly interested in him. Akari's blood may flow through half of him, but the other half is a nobody from heaven knows where. And yet…"

"Wait! Ayato has nothing to do with this!"

"…Indeed. So long as you understand that." Though Lamina Mortis kept his voice cool and calm throughout, Haruka detected—if only for a second—an undoubtedly intentional glistening of something terrible.

"…Just what are you trying to achieve?"

She only barely managed to wring the words out of her throat.

"Oh, it's nothing too complicated," Lamina Mortis said lightly as he crossed his legs. "Only a second Invertia."

*

"A second Invertia…?!" Helga exclaimed, rising to her feet. Her countenance had turned sterner than Ayato had ever seen before.

And she wasn't alone. All of them, even Claudia, were left speechless, wearing expressions of utter shock.

"N-n-no, they couldn't…," Julis murmured, the words of dismay almost too low to catch. Ayato didn't need to hear the rest to share her reaction.

The Invertia was the greatest disaster in human history, a catastrophe that became a turning point for all mankind. It had swept away the past, changing the world beyond recognition, and brought untold tragedy in exchange for the gifts of mana and manadite.

Not even the integrated enterprise foundations should be able to bring about a second such calamity, no matter how godlike their power…

At that moment, a memory suddenly flashed before Ayato's eyes.

It was during the school fair the previous year, when he had first met Xinglou Fan, Jie Long Seventh Institute's student council president.

"The Invertia was no natural disaster. It was caused, intentionally, by someone."

That was what she had said.

And: that there was nothing to stop it from happening again.

"I can't blame you if you don't believe me. I couldn't believe it at first, either… But I could tell, just by looking at him, that he wasn't joking. I don't know whether he can actually do it or how, for that matter, but he's definitely going to try. I can feel it in my bones. What he wants is destruction." Haruka paused there to catch her breath before pursing her lips. "And I also thought, if he's going to try to cause another Invertia, then I had to stop him, and I had to do it by myself… What other choice did I have? I mean, no one would believe me with a story like that…"

She was no doubt right about that, Ayato thought with a grimace. Even if she went to the police or somehow managed to get word to the upper echelons of the foundations, it was hard to believe that they would be willing to accept what she told them: that an unidentified masked man was involved in a conspiracy to wreak havoc and destruction on such a scale.

"But this Lamina Mortis was clearly much stronger than me. It was obvious enough I'd have no chance of beating him in a fight… So I decided to go along with him. If I could get more information, if I could manage to interrupt his plans somehow… But I guess he probably expected me to try to do all that even before he invited me."

"...Probably," Ayato murmured in agreement, gaze downcast.

At least he knew now why she had disappeared. He might not have been able to fully accept it on an emotional level, but he suspected that had he been in her position, he would probably have made the same choice.

"But," she continued, her voice warm, "before all that, there was one thing I had to do. I had to protect you, Ayato."

"Me...?" Ayato looked up, only to see a sad smile rise to his sister's lips.

"I asked him, Lamina Mortis, for a chance to see you one last time before I went with him. On the condition that I didn't say anything about his plans. Not that I had any intention of bringing it up anyway—I mean, if I told you, you'd come chasing after me, right? You were already strong enough to do so."

"—! So that's why you sealed my power away...?"

"Yes. To stop you from coming after me." Haruka's voice possessed a complex mixture of anguish and affection. "But I knew I should still give you room to choose for yourself once you'd grown up a bit more—if I wasn't able to come back to you, if you still thought the same way about me."

"So that's why Ayato's seal was unlocked in stages," Saya murmured to herself, frowning.

"Yes. I set the conditions for unlocking them at the minimum level that I thought you would need to reach before confronting Lamina Mortis. The first would be released when you found something you needed to achieve at all costs... I know it was a while back, but do you remember what we spoke about that night?"

"...Of course." The memory from his childhood flashed through his mind.

Ignoring his father's instructions, he had gone and joined the other students from the dojo.

Even now, his sister's words that day, and his own response, were engraved in his soul.

"The second would be released once you found friends that you trusted from the bottom of your heart."

That one had been unlocked during his semifinal match at the Phoenix, against the Li twins from Jie Long, when he finally understood that he couldn't just become Julis's strength, but that he needed her to become his, too.

"And the third one... The third would be released once your strength surpassed my own."

"...Ah, so that was it."

The final stage of the seal had been released during the championship match of the Gryps, in the middle of his duel against Ernest.

In that case, it sounded like he had finally caught up to his sister.

"You would need to pass all three hurdles before you'd be strong enough to face Lamina Mortis, I thought."

"I'm sorry, Haruka. I...I hadn't even passed the first one before coming here..."

When Ayato first came to Asterisk, he still hadn't been able to break through the first seal, even when mustering all his strength. He had still been, it seemed, far from what Haruka had envisioned.

"There's no need to apologize!" Claudia called out, rushing to Ayato's defense. "I invited you here for my own selfish reasons!" Her countenance and voice betrayed an unusual depth of emotion.

"Thank you, Claudia. But I still decided to come here on my own..."

"That doesn't change the fact that I—"

"Enough already, you two!" Haruka interrupted, no doubt sensing that neither Ayato nor Claudia would give ground to the other. "What matters is that the seal is gone now, right?"

"But Haruka! I...?!"

But... Right. That wasn't what he really needed to tell her.

That day, he could clearly put his feelings into words.

"Then, I'm going to protect you, too, sis! That's what I have to do!"

But he hadn't been able to keep his word.

Perhaps there was no helping it. Judging from what Haruka had said, he wouldn't have been strong enough at the time to make any difference.

But it wasn't the words he'd spoken that pained him so much.

As a wave of regret washed over him, he clenched his fists so hard that he feared he might draw blood.

He understood now: What he had to do was add something else to the strength he already had. And once he'd come to Asterisk, he had found that something in the form of an obstinate, kindhearted princess.

He had to be strong—not for himself, but for someone else's protection.

That certainly wasn't unrelated to what he had said to his sister that day, but it wasn't exactly the same thing, either. To protect someone, to be their strength, meant that one had to first probe to the bottom of one's own inner strength.

What he'd said back then had been more like a wish. Looking back, he couldn't help but feel chagrined at just how naive he had been.

And yet—

"You did well, Ayato," Haruka said, stroking his head gently.

That was all.

She said no more than that, but Ayato felt something deep inside his chest, something that had been there for longer than he could remember, begin to thaw.

"...Yeah."

As he closed his eyes, that now-distant summer night rose up before him once more.

Haruka's voice now was just as firm and as kind as he remembered.

"Um, ahem." Helga let out a feigned cough.

Ayato, embarrassed, sat up straight. He felt the heat rising to his cheeks as he realized just how warmly Julis and the others were staring at him.

"...Sorry, but I need to hear the rest of what happened," Helga said guiltily as she turned her keen gaze back to Haruka. "Can you confirm the details of this plan you were talking about? I need to know how it ended."

"Ah, all right... It'll take a while to go into all the details, and I don't really understand it all myself, but okay. How it ended... I was able to put a stop to it. I think." She spoke matter-of-factly, her chin resting in her hand.

"Put a stop to it? Just like that…?" Ayato repeated in bewilderment.

"No, not 'just like that,' of course. I wouldn't have been able to destroy the rocket without the Ser Veresta. And Ecknardt was unbelievably strong. And even though I was able to put a stop to it, that didn't stop them from catching me. We were out at sea, so there was nowhere to run…"

"Wait, you were out at sea? And what's this about a rocket?" Helga interrupted. "It sounds like I'm going to have a lot of questions, but let's start with this Ecknardt fellow. Who is he?"

"He was with Lamina Mortis, I guess. Mortis was responsible for leading the plan, but I got the impression that it was Ecknardt who really put it all together."

"What kind of person is he?" Helga pressed.

Haruka, however, shook her head. "He wasn't a person."

"…What?" Helga snapped, furrowing her brow. "You don't mean that metaphorically?"

"No. He looked human, like a young man… But he wasn't. He was something else, a different kind of existence."

A different kind of existence.

It wasn't the kind of story that most people would be prepared to believe, but Ayato himself knew of at least two others who matched that description.

"How do I put this? It was like mana itself had taken the form of a person… Anyway, the gist of the plan was to send Ecknardt to the moon. That's what the floating launch platform and the rocket were for."

"Th-the moon…?!" Kirin stammered. "But I thought we lost that technology centuries ago…?"

From what Ayato had read, humanity had indeed possessed the ability to land on the moon, at least up until the Invertia occurred.

Now, however, while humanity had made great strides in the sciences thanks to advances in meteoric engineering, space development was the one field that seemed to have regressed. Perhaps because very little mana existed in space, present-day research into space technology both began and ended with the deployment of satellites and the like.

"That isn't exactly right," Saya corrected them. "The Japan Aerospace Exploration Agency was planning a manned mission to the moon a short while back. But that ended up, well…" She trailed off there, her expression turning suddenly mournful.

"Yes, I'm familiar with what happened," Claudia said, picking up the story for her. "That manned lunar mission was canceled after a massive explosion at the testing facility. Given the number of casualties, I suppose it couldn't be helped."

At this, Haruka's expression clouded over. "I'm pretty sure that was *their* doing. Lamina Mortis and the others."

"What?!"

"I overheard him say that the engine was stolen from the JAXA…"

"But that all happened over a decade ago," Claudia murmured, unable to conceal her surprise.

In that case, Lamina Mortis and his associates must have been planning this for quite some time.

"Assuming Ecknardt reached the moon, how exactly was he planning to cause another Invertia?" Helga asked.

"I don't know the details, but it sounded like he was going to use a large urm-manadite crystal," Haruka answered.

"Hrm." Helga bit her lip in frustration. "I don't know how we could verify that…"

She might have been the strongest Strega in Asterisk's history, but not even she could travel to the moon.

"Just before they could put it all into motion, I managed to sneak aboard the launch platform and destroy the rocket. I ended up fighting Ecknardt, but beating him took all my strength, and the others caught me. Ah! I destroyed the launch platform, too, so the wreckage might still be on the ocean floor!" Haruka paused there, opening a world map in an air-window from the terminal by her bed and zooming in on a part of the ocean near the equator.

"I'm grateful for the information, but unfortunately, Stjarnagarm has no authority outside the city. It'll be difficult for us to investigate. More importantly, though, what happened to Ecknardt?"

"Well, when I finally managed to land a blow, he kind of shattered, like a piece of glass..."

"Like a piece of glass...? So he really wasn't human...?" Julis murmured in a low voice.

"I was ready to face the consequences, but Lamina Mortis stopped them from killing me. They detained me somewhere for a while, then he told me they'd make me join them unless I could beat him in a duel..."

"The Eclipse, you mean...?" Ayato asked.

Haruka nodded. "I knew I'd lose, but I used the opportunity to seal away his power. And then I put another seal on myself, so that I wouldn't be able to remove the one that I'd put on him."

The abilities of Stregas and Dantes didn't necessarily dispel even upon the death of their user (although such abilities weren't uncommon, either). Given the seal that Haruka had put on him, Lamina Mortis probably didn't want to risk killing her.

"Phew... I guess that's the short version of it all." Haruka breathed out a heavy sigh as she stretched her arms.

"That's... You really are amazing, Haru..." Those were the only words that Ayato could find at first after listening to her story to the end.

"I'd already heard about you from Ayato...but you certainly match his descriptions, that's for sure."

"You really messed them up!"

"A very impressive accomplishment!"

"You're just like Ayato!"

Julis, Saya, Claudia, and Kirin, respectively, couldn't hide their admiration for her, either.

"All right, I think I've got a rough understanding of what happened. I'll admit, it's a little difficult to believe, so I'll have to get you to go over it all again in more detail soon." With that, Helga rose to her feet.

"Ah, Helga," Haruka called out after her, her next words leaving Ayato even more stunned than he already was: "If it's all right with you—can I join Stjarnagarm?"

CHAPTER 4
MADIATH MESA

Akari returned to the customer who had told her about the Eclipse, announcing that she would compete—along with a friend—and was given a time and place to wait for further instructions.

It was one o'clock in the middle of the night, amid the rubble of the redevelopment area.

A masked, suited man stood before them in the run-down building, his features highlighted by the moonlight leaking in through the decaying roof in the run-down building. He couldn't have looked more suspicious.

"...In short, with you both joining us, tonight's battle royal will have twelve contestants in total."

In an unassuming and polite tone of voice, the man explained to them both how the Eclipse worked. For a representative of a secretive underground organization, he seemed surprisingly thoughtful.

"In principle, there are no rules in the Eclipse. You may use any weapon that you wish, and there are no penalties for how you fight. The match is over when one side is no longer able to compete, but please understand that we cannot be held accountable for the outcome—not even if one party or the other should lose their life."

In other words, it was possible to die in this tournament. For Madiath, who had spent the better part of his life fighting under the same conditions, that wasn't a major concern—but Akari, he suspected, would be less pleased to hear it.

Or so he had thought, but when he looked toward her, he saw that she was merely wearing her usual ambiguous smile.

"...Don't tell me you're used to this kind of thing?" he whispered, leaning close.

Akari, however, gave her head a slight shake. "No, I've never had to bet my life on something like this before," she replied in a voice as soft as his own. "But I'm fine with it. This life of mine isn't worth much to begin with anyway."

Madiath could hardly contain his surprise, only realizing after the fact that his mouth had fallen open a fraction. Akari continued to defy his expectations.

Yes, this was indeed an interesting person.

He had never met anyone quite like her before.

"It's almost time. I will have to take temporary possession of your mobile devices in order to maintain secrecy. I trust this will be acceptable?"

"I understand."

"Fine."

The two of them handed their mobiles over as instructed.

The man gave them a composed nod. "Very good. Please, come this way. The elevator will take you down to the stage."

"Elevator? Where...?" Madiath examined his surroundings, but there was nothing amid the ruins that so much as resembled such a thing.

Before the man could answer, however, their surroundings changed completely, in the blink of an eye.

"!"

"This is...!"

This time, even Akari covered her mouth in astonishment.

That was only to be expected. A second ago, they had been standing in a dilapidated room lit only by the beams of wan moonlight sneaking in through the cracks above. Now they found themselves in a dank, windowless cellar.

No, it isn't our surroundings that just changed...

"...We've probably been transported somewhere else," Akari whispered.

"Yeah... I find I have to agree."

In other words, they had been teleported to a place they weren't familiar with.

"I've heard of something like this before. Apparently, Le Wolfe has an Orga Lux capable of teleporting things across preset coordinates..."

Akari let out an impressed murmur. "Huh, that does sound possible."

And if that was in fact the case, there was a good chance that an Orga Lux user, or even Le Wolfe itself, was involved in this Eclipse.

With the exception of a cold, silver-colored door directly in front of them, the room was completely empty.

"I guess this is the elevator, then?"

"Looks like it."

Madiath pushed the button on the panel beside it, whereupon the door immediately slid open to reveal a space about twenty-two square yards in size.

Having come this far, they entered the elevator together, a peculiar sense of unease falling over them as it descended ever downward.

"...Are you sure you're all right with this?" Akari asked him all of a sudden.

"Huh? What do you mean?"

"With getting dragged into this. It's going to be dangerous. I mean, I'm glad you're helping me, but I don't know how to thank you."

"There's no need for thanks... And haven't we already been over this?" he replied with a slight grin.

Akari merely frowned back at him, as if she couldn't quite accept his response, but said nothing more.

The truth was that Madiath wasn't looking to receive anything from her in return.

Of course, that didn't mean that he was helping her out of the goodness of his heart.

He simply hadn't met anyone until now whom he could genuinely say interested him. Whether people were good or bad, strong or weak, friendly or antagonistic, he tended to think of them only in terms of variables that affected his own environment. He thought no more or less of any specific individual.

In his world, there was no one else but himself—and that had been enough.

Until he met Akari, that was.

"I guess we're here, then."

The elevator came to a stop, its silver-colored door sliding open.

No sooner had they stepped out than they were confronted by dazzling lights and the cheers of the audience.

It wasn't, however, the same kind of passion and excitement that one normally found at the Festa—these voices were darker, baser, more wicked in nature.

"And now at last, our final contestants, Seidoukan's number forty-four, Madiath Mesa, alias Ravana, and Akari Yachigusa, also from Seidoukan Academy! I'm looking forward to seeing which of our heroes gathered here tonight manages to rise to the top!" The fevered, high-pitched voice—no doubt that of the announcer—echoed across the stage.

It was an unusually wide stage, hexagonal in shape. In each of its six corners, there were large pillars, which housed elevators, towering high into the darkness. The audience seating seemed to encircle the stage, but given the lighting and the difference in elevation, they couldn't be seen from down where Madiath and Akari were standing.

There were no obstacles or the like to be found on the stage—only the figures of ten other contestants silently appraising them.

"...This is it? Talk about disappointing," Madiath murmured as he summed them up in turn.

For an illicit battle tournament operating under the nose of the Festa, he had been expecting something a little...*more.*

Of course, the Vigridhr itself was no match for the Festa, but even so, those who took part in it were strong enough that unwary or unskilled entrants could easily find themselves killed. Those who participated in it needed an iron resolve—to keep living, even if that meant death for one's opponent.

But Madiath's opponents now, the ten other individuals standing at the other corners of the stage, seemed to lack that sense of desperation. Frankly speaking, they came across as little more than amateurish.

Judging by their appearance, they were all students at another one of Asterisk's six schools, but it was clear enough at first glance that none of them were skilled enough to reach a high position in the rankings.

That being the case, Madiath reflected ruefully, Akari would no doubt have been fine taking care of everyone by herself.

"With that, let's get tonight's first match under way! Begin!"

The announcer's voice still resounding through the chamber, Madiath took note of their closest opponent, a student from Allekant aiming an assault rifle–shaped Lux in their direction.

But before he could fire—

"Freeze," Akari murmured from behind, a wave of mana bursting forth and interrupting his movements.

"Huh…?!" The Allekant student, flustered, kept pulling the trigger over and over—but far from being able to launch an attack, his Lux's manadite core lost all power, extinguished.

And that wasn't all.

"Wh-what's going on…?!"

"Impossible! My mana won't respond…!"

"You mean you can't use your abilities?!"

The voices of the students fighting all across the stage rose up in panic.

Even the audience seemed to be overcome with bewilderment.

Madiath, grinning, let out a light whistle. "Well now… That *is* impressive."

"What do we have here? Is this Akari Yachigusa's ability at work? Word has it that she has the power to completely nullify the effects of mana! Pretty crazy, huh?"

As the announcer, no doubt having obtained data on each of the contestants, explained the situation, a wave of shock spread across both stage and audience alike.

That was understandable. Not only could such an ability essentially incapacitate Stregas and Dantes, it also deactivated any nearby Luxes—and there was no reason, at least theoretically, why it wouldn't be effective against an Orga Lux, either.

Of course, that meant she wouldn't be able to use any Luxes herself. Nor, for that matter, would Madiath.

But that didn't matter.

"Now, then."

"Gah…!"

Madiath took down the Allekant student, still struggling to reactivate his Lux, with a powerful blow to the abdomen.

If this was the best his opponents had to offer, then he wouldn't even need weapons to win.

Checking behind him, he caught sight of Akari turning the tables on a student from Jie Long, using the flat of her hand as a blade.

The other contestants, having seen what they were both capable of, began to fall back.

The match may have been a battle royal, but the contestants were already beginning to organize themselves into groups. This was a common strategy—and indeed, Madiath and Akari had been fighting as a tag team from the very beginning.

In a battle royal, it was common to work together with one's opponents to take down the most formidable or troublesome parties first. As such, the others all seemed to have set their sights on Akari, but having seen both hers and Madiath's combat ability firsthand, they were clearly becoming unnerved.

Such hastily constructed teams, however, were seldom able to capitalize on their advantage in numbers. If one member was willing to sacrifice themselves, they might be able to create an opening for the others to take advantage of, but no one wanted to be the first to move. In a battle royal, the ultimate aim was one's own survival, and so the members of such teams tended to get their priorities in reverse.

That was the case this very moment. Each of Madiath's and Akari's opponents kept glancing at one another nervously, none willing to take the first risk.

The audience, having quickly grown impatient, began to shower down jeers and abuse—and yet, still, none of their opponents showed any sign of moving.

"...Good grief. Talk about boring."

If this was how it was going to play out, then he had no choice but to finish things himself.

But before Madiath could launch into an assault of his own—

"Well now! This is *a problem! It looks like our contestants are all unwilling to fight! Most unsatisfying! But not to worry! Rest assured we won't let the most exciting show on Earth go to waste! We have something special prepared for moments like this!"*

As the announcer's cries faded into silence, a large hole began to open in the center of the stage, from which the figures of two men stepped forth.

The first belonged to a young man dressed in a Jie Long uniform and wearing a half-broken wolf's mask.

The second was a tall, emaciated man in the prime of his life, garbed in an everyday kimono and wielding an oversized sword, at least six and a half feet long.

"Here we are! Our professional fighters who you know so well, Zakir, the famed Scarmask, and Ryoue Arato, the Fallen Swordsman!"

As the announcer called out the names of the new challengers, the crowd's boos changed at once into a roar of frenzied excitement.

"Hah, I guess this was the plan all along."

The two newcomers were clearly of an altogether different caliber than the other contestants.

It looked like the first round, the battle royal, was merely an appetizer, with these two hunting down whoever was left standing for the main course. The Vigridhr followed the same formula every now and then, too.

"Do you know those two?" Madiath called out to Akari.

"Yes. They're both criminals, and famously violent ones at that. Zakir is the former top agent of Jie Long's intelligence organization Gaishi, and Ryoue Arato is the third person to hold the title of Kensei." Akari spoke without hesitation, neither her voice nor her countenance betraying any hint of fear.

"H-hold on! What the hell is this?!"

"What are Scarmask and Kensei doing here…?!"

Their original opponents all began to raise their voices in protest.

However—

"…Pathetic."

Ryoue's blade seemed to flicker through the air, casting up a spray of blood as he cut through the three contestants closest to him. His skill with that custom weapon of his was nothing short of remarkable.

"Heh-heh… Don't say that, Ryoue. This'll just make their screams all the juicier!" Zakir announced, standing beside him as a bestial grin spread across the exposed half of his face.

As he spoke, a student from Le Wolfe circled around behind him. He appeared to be one of the more competent of the original entrants and was succeeding, it seemed, in concealing his presence. However—

"Like this," Zakir said with a smirk, striking backward with the tip of his hand without so much as glancing over his shoulder.

"Gyaaaaaaaaaah!"

The next moment, the Le Wolfe student fell backward with a terrible scream, crimson blood gushing onto the ground surrounding him.

"Don't worry," Zakir said, laughing, his gore-coated hand charged with an incredible amount of prana. "It's flashy, but not enough to kill you. I just carved out a nice piece of useless flesh."

"So he's put everything he's got into offense," Madiath murmured to himself.

That wasn't the kind of thing that any normal person could hope to pull off. Either Zakir had a natural mastery over his prana or he had built his way up to this point through endless training.

"What a horrible thing to do...," Akari whispered as she looked on at the harrowing sight, but her words seemed somehow cold, almost lacking in sympathy. She may have had a kind, gentle disposition, but even now, she held herself at a distance from her surroundings.

It was that very fact that had first sparked Madiath's interest in her.

She had called herself an unwanted child, but what kind of life must she have led to live so detached from everything?

"There's our professional fighters for you, folks! Just watch how they spice things up!"

With Zakir and Ryoue having entered the stage, the spectacle was turning into one of carnage, one that had the audience hanging on tenterhooks.

While Madiath had guessed as much, this was what the audience of the Eclipse had come to see.

Zakir and Ryoue took care of the remaining contestants in a matter of minutes before finally turning their gazes toward Madiath and Akari for the first time.

"Heh, time for the main dish... I've been looking forward to you two."

"...Disappear..."

Only the four of them remained standing—Madiath, Akari, Zakir, and Ryoue.

"I've fought swordsmen before, so I'll take Ryoue Arato," Akari began.

Madiath, however, held out a hand to stop her. "Don't. Leave them both to me."

"Huh...? But Madiath..."

Akari's unique ability was highly effective against Stregas and Dantes, but it was completely useless against those who fought empty-handed, like most students from Jie Long, or those who used more traditional weapons. Zakir and Ryoue both fell into those categories.

That probably wasn't a coincidence. The organizers of the Eclipse had no doubt selected the two of them knowing full well her strengths and weaknesses. She was skilled in close combat—Madiath would grant her that—but she was nowhere near the level of the two opponents facing them now.

"I'll handle them. Besides, you've still got something left to do, right?" Madiath said as he stepped in Zakir's and Ryoue's direction.

"Huh? What's this? You think you can fight us alone or something?"

"Insolence…!"

Perhaps thinking he was trying to make fools of them, Zakir and Ryoue glared at him, their eyes burning with savagery.

Madiath, on the other hand, said nothing, merely continuing to walk slowly toward them, one step after the other.

He was already within Ryoue's range.

And with his next step, he was within Zakir's, too.

At that moment—

"Pò!"

"Yah!"

Zakir came hurtling toward him with an outstretched palm from his right, while Ryoue lunged forward with a wide slash from the left.

They were rapid, sharp, unerringly precise blows—but nothing more than that.

"Huh?!"

He quickened his pace ever so slightly, deflecting Ryoue's blade with the back of his hand, while at the same time countering Zakir's strike and launching into a quick flurry of punches directed into his chin.

"Ugh!"

With Ryoue, having spun halfway around due to his failed slash, now vulnerable, Madiath then moved to drive his elbow into his lower back.

After pivoting rapidly from one opponent to the other, Madiath now strode calmly into the center of the stage—when Zakir and Ryoue both crumbled soundlessly to the ground behind him.

"…Huuuuuh?!"

The audience, so shocked by what had just happened, was utterly silent, as if they had been doused with water. The vast majority of them probably hadn't even realized just what he had done.

"Now then, Akari!" he beckoned toward her as she glimpsed over his shoulder.

At last, that vaguely bitter smile of hers was no more, her eyes staring at him wide in surprise. Madiath, still not used to seeing her act so expressive, couldn't help but feel a touch of pride.

"I wasn't expecting that," she said meekly. "They looked so strong, but to think they fell so easily..."

"It's nothing. They were weak, that's all. More importantly..." He paused there, spreading his arms out wide.

Akari blinked at him for a moment, before a strange smile—one that he hadn't seen before—rose to her lips. "Something left to do, huh?" she murmured, her shoulders trembling with amusement as she lifted her arm into the air—and poked him lightly in the forehead.

"Argh, I've been beaten," he said flatly as he lowered himself theatrically to lie facedown on the ground.

After a long, drawn-out moment, the audience, having realized what exactly had just happened, began to rain down a storm of abuse.

*

"Looks like you got your prize money safe and sound."

"Yes. Thank you, Madiath," Akari said with a relieved smile, before bowing deeply toward him. "This is for you."

"I told you, there's no need for thanks," Madiath said with a chuckle as the two of them began to make their way out of the redevelopment area.

It was almost dawn. Akari, the winner, had been allowed to return to the surface on the elevator they had used to descend to the stage. Madiath and the other defeated contestants, however, were taken down the hole that had appeared in the middle of the stage, and so it took him a good length of time to make his way back.

If he had been the winner, he would probably have just gone straight back to the academy, but Akari, it seemed, had decided to wait.

The area beneath the stage had been set up like some kind of prison. It brought back unpleasant memories of his time in the Vigridhr, but fortunately, there didn't seem to be anybody forced to live down there as he had been. There, he and the other defeated contestants were awarded a small sum for their participation. Those with serious injuries, however, received the bare minimum of medical treatment—payment for which was deducted from their reward at an exorbitant rate.

The person who handed Madiath his payment also had a few words for him: "If you're going to do that, try to make it look a bit more natural next time."

Madiath's response was simple: "Don't worry. There won't be a next time."

Of course, giving the audience a natural defeat was, after all, his specialty—and so he had lost the way he had on purpose. If he had to give a reason for having done what he did...perhaps it had something to do with the fact that this was the first time in several years he had ended up taking a match seriously.

In any event, he had to admit that it wasn't like him.

In fact, it wasn't like him at all to take things as seriously as he had been doing of late—whether that was going out with Akari or taking part in the Eclipse.

Still, he didn't dislike this new side of himself.

Out of nowhere, Akari, walking by his side, asked him a question: "Madiath, why are you being so kind to me?"

"Because I'm interested in you," he answered honestly.

Akari tilted her head, her cheeks turning pink. "That's... Do you mean, romantically?"

"Huh...," Madiath returned vacantly; it had thrown him. "Ah... I wonder. Unfortunately, I'm not so clear on that myself."

That was the honest truth—he himself couldn't say exactly what light it was he saw her in.

"I see... What a coincidence. I feel the same way."

"You do?"

"I don't really know what it means to love someone. I mean, if you can't even love yourself, how are you supposed to fall in love with someone else?" Akari said with her usual vaguely sad smile.

"That's—"

But before Madiath could properly respond, both he and Akari came to a sudden stop.

Something was waiting for them in the darkness.

"Oh-ho! Things have gotten a little awkward, haven't they, children?"

The figure had the shape of a young woman, but to Madiath's eyes, it didn't appear human. She was pretty in a way that seemed to disguise her years, with long, black hair and loose-fitting Chinese-style clothes, but Madiath could sense a maturity and depth of experience that belied her appearance.

"The Ban'yuu Tenra..."

"...Xiaoyuan Wang."

The name of the figure in front of them spilled from both of their mouths simultaneously.

Even Madiath, who had spent his childhood in the Vigridhr estranged from the affairs of the world, knew of this woman. Xiaoyuan Wang was the only person in all of Asterisk's history to win a grand slam at the Festa, and now she ruled over Jie Long. From what he understood, she had become a teacher at the institute after graduating and now dedicated herself to nurturing her students.

"Oh, I didn't mean to disturb you. I've actually just come back from watching the Eclipse. Though it shames me to admit it, Zakir was an unworthy student." As she spoke, Xiaoyuan's gentle smile and tone of voice remained completely unchanging.

"Don't tell me the great Ban'yuu Tenra is here to take revenge on us?" Madiath glowered when a cold chill suddenly ran down his spine.

She looks like a genuine monster... I guess it's true what they say—you can find just about anything in this city.

In all his years, Madiath had never seen anyone as manifestly powerful as her.

"Fret not. I wouldn't debase myself like that. I just wanted to confirm something for myself."

"Confirm what, exactly...?"

Before he could finish speaking, however, Xiaoyuan had somehow moved directly in front of him.

"Wha—?!"

"Madiath!"

She appeared within range of him with unbelievable speed, sending her fist lunging toward him so fast that he barely had enough time to catch it over the sound of Akari's desperate cry. The surface of the road began to break beneath him as he stood his ground against a successive wave of strikes, the cracks radiating out all the way to the dilapidated buildings on either side.

"Just as I thought... So you can parry that, too, can you...?"

"I don't know what your problem is, but isn't this a bit much...?" Taken aback by her overpowering physical strength, Madiath only barely managed to hold her small fists at bay.

"Oh-ho! This is just a warm-up!" Xiaoyuan replied, a dauntless grin rising to her lips, when—

"Oh *dear*... Is that *it*?" Finally, she relented, leaping backward to put some space between the two of them. "This is unfortunate. As I feared, you have talent, but you lack savagery. Most distasteful."

"...You come at me out of nowhere, and then you criticize my fighting?" Madiath demanded, feeling vaguely aggrieved. "And what's this about savagery?"

"Savagery is the wellspring of one's fighting spirit, born from one's competitive instincts. Anger, hate, envy, desire—the impulse to destroy your opponent arises from these primal passions. The strong burn bright with their savagery, to one extent or another. But not you. Most ironic, given your appellation, Ravana. You're no Demon King."

"You're a talker, huh?" Madiath remarked, but inwardly, he couldn't help but be impressed by how well Xiaoyuan had read him.

Anyway, it wasn't like he had picked the name for himself.

"There might still be time to make something more appetizing out of you...but I don't see much point. I'll be waiting for you to discover your inner savagery," Xiaoyuan said with a wave of her hand—and just like that, she was gone, vanished as if into thin air.

"What the heck is that supposed to mean...?"

"I wonder...?" Akari murmured, clearly unsure how to respond.

At the time, Madiath had yet to understand the depth of meaning that lay behind Xiaoyuan's words—but it wouldn't be long until he found out.

*

The following day, in the student council room at Seidoukan Academy—

"No, no, you fought magnificently, the both of you. I'm impressed, truly," the student council president said from his position by the window, flashing a stiff smile to both Madiath and Akari.

Despite his words, however, his eyes clearly burned with indignation.

"Who would have thought that you were both harboring such talent? To defeat Scarmask and the Fallen Swordsman like that... I don't know how I missed it. My eyes must be failing me."

"I'm shocked as well," Madiath retorted. "I wouldn't have expected our esteemed student council president to have anything to do with that shady little enterprise."

Far from responding to this provocation, however, the student council president merely returned to his seat, letting out a composed sigh.

As rotten as he might have been, he had still earned his position and so would hardly be incompetent.

Whether he was fully competent or not, though, was another matter entirely.

"Let's put the fact that you weren't forthcoming about your abilities aside for now. Everyone has their own private circumstances, after all…myself included, of course." The student council president folded his hands, looking sternly at Madiath and Akari from across his desk. "Madiath. For now, I want you to take part in this year's Phoenix. I won't take no for an answer. You *are* living off one of our special scholarships, after all."

"…Fine."

Every case was different, but most students who enrolled on special scholarships were bound by certain contractual obligations, which they didn't have the liberty to ignore. Participation in the Festa, when instructed by their school, was one of those.

If he were to break that contract now, he would almost certainly find himself back in the hull of that cramped, gloomy airship—and he wasn't about to let that happen.

"Very good. There aren't any particularly notable stars taking part this year. So as long as you keep doing what you did yesterday, you shouldn't have any problem taking the crown." His mood perhaps lightening, the student council president flashed him a smile considerably warmer than before. "Now then, Akari Yachigusa."

"…Yes?" Akari, until now staring down at her feet in silence, answered softly. Her expression was as veiled as usual, but she was clearly sullen.

"Your ability to halt the flow of mana is extraordinary. Looking over our data, it appears that we already knew about it…but it says here that *you can't control it very well*? And that you have no fighting experience nor confidence in your capacity to defend yourself."

"…That's correct."

"Oh?" The student council president raised an eyebrow in feigned surprise. "Enlighten me."

"Once I activate my ability, I'm unable to dispel it when I want. In the past, I couldn't even control when it activated. And just like your data says, I've never been taught how to fight."

There was probably no lie in Akari's response.

Judging by what Madiath had seen, her close-combat ability was quite high, but her movements and techniques didn't appear to be in line with any particular style.

Having said that, she clearly wasn't an amateur.

"In other words, you taught yourself?"

"Yes...by watching others."

"Even better! Let's say it was that natural ability of yours that pulled you through the Eclipse."

"That was all thanks to Madiath—"

But before Akari could explain further, the student council president rose to his feet. "I would very much like for you to team up with Madiath in the Phoenix as his tag partner," he declared.

Madiath had expected from the moment that he and Akari had been called to this office together that it might come to this.

"...I'm sorry," Akari replied with a sad smile, her voice wavering, as if she were on the verge of crying. "I can't do that."

"Hmm..." The student council president appeared disappointed for a brief moment but quickly regained his composure. "Unlike with Madiath, I can't force you to compete. This is a request, and you're free to turn it down—but I would like to hear, at least, your reason for doing so."

"I... My family told me not to bring attention to myself."

"The Yachigusa family? One of the oldest in the country, no? I've heard a bit about them. They do seem to be a bit stuck in their ways... In Europe, at least, the upper classes have started to see the advantages to be gained from letting Genestella be Genestella..." The student council president let out a deep sigh as he shrugged before flashing her another smile. "But are *you* really so concerned by what these outmoded relatives of yours think?"

"Huh...?" At this, Akari looked up at him.

"The one you're really concerned about...is your mother, no?"

At that moment, Akari's feigned composure shattered. "—!"

"...Don't you think you're pushing it a bit?" Madiath demanded with an edge, taking a step forward.

The student council president turned pale as he slunk away. "S-sorry, but it's my job...!"

As he spoke, several figures suddenly appeared around him, as if to shield him from attack. Their appearance would have been sudden, but Madiath had sensed their presence in the room from the moment he entered.

"So you're Shadowstar."

The five students, each wearing deep hoods that concealed their faces, appeared to know their way around a fight.

That was to be expected of Seidoukan Academy's secretive intelligence and operations organization.

All of a sudden, the student standing at the forefront of the group, who carried himself with the most confidence, removed his hood.

Staring back at Madiath was his own face. "Ooh, look who we have here!" his mirror said with a fearless grin.

Great… A copyist…

Madiath had fought against a great many opponents during his days in the Vigridhr. Among them, the number of Stregas and Dantes with copy abilities was by no means inconsiderable. The question was always how accurate they could pull it off, and under what conditions.

"Let's leave it at that, Lantana," the student council president said.

The man—Lantana—put on his hood again, returning to his previous position.

"Do you understand, Madiath? I didn't mean to threaten Miss Yachigusa here. Quite the opposite. I'm trying to help."

"To help?"

"If I could convince the Yachigusa family, and Akari's mother in particular, wouldn't that solve all our problems?" the student council president explained.

"You'd convince my mother…?"

"Well, not me, strictly speaking—Galaxy would."

"…" At this, Akari fell silent, deep in thought.

Certainly, it would be difficult for anyone—even an esteemed upper-class family—to turn down an offer from an integrated enterprise foundation.

"…I'm grateful, but I don't want to burden my mother any more than I already have…," Akari replied, but it was clear she was still in two minds.

Perhaps noticing her indecision, the student council president refused to relent. "Hah, don't worry about that. We won't burden her. Think of it as a negotiation. I'm sure they'll understand so long as we politely and firmly lay out our arguments. If they still say no, well, that will be the end of it."

Madiath, on the other hand, found himself at a crossroads.

It would be easy enough for him to put a stop to the present conversation, but he had no idea how hard he should push it. This clearly wasn't the kind of problem that would be solved by an outsider's meddling, but this situation included him, too, and he found himself wavering over whose side he should take.

He, who until now had viewed others only through the lens of his own interests, was unable to decide whether to act or not.

"...Will you promise not to force her?" Akari asked in a faint, trembling voice.

With this, the student council president held out his hand. "Of course. It's a promise."

Akari nervously accepted it with her own.

In the end, all Madiath could do was stand there and watch on in paralyzed silence.

CHAPTER 5
DREAMS OF THE LINDVOLUS

"Ah, I love spring! It's almost time for the school fair again..."

Today, as with almost every other weekday at Seidoukan, the cafeteria was bustling with students. In the center of that mass of activity sat Eishirou, nibbling on a croquette and looking nostalgic.

"Are you not doing anything special this time around?" Ayato, sitting across from him, asked over his plate of pasta.

"What, when I worked so hard last time?"

During the last school fair, Eishirou's newspaper club had been one of the main organizers of a major event and were busy practically every day.

"That was an exception. This year, we're just planning to do a couple of interviews. I mean, the club prez—well, the former club prez—has already gone and graduated. So now we're just passing one peaceful day after another." Behind those words was a trace of sadness in Eishirou's voice.

"Forget about that, Amagiri," Lester demanded from his seat by Eishirou's side. "What's this about you not entering the Lindvolus?" He was resting his chin on his hands, the scraps of the hamburger that he had just eaten laying before him on the table.

"Ah, yeah. I don't really have any other wishes that I want granted. And besides, I don't want to get in Julis's way."

"*Tch!* And here I was thinking I'd have a chance to take you both down." Lester scowled.

"Speaking of which… You seem to be working yourself pretty hard lately, Lester," Eishirou remarked.

Unlike his roommate, Eishirou, Ayato didn't have many opportunities to meet Lester, but it was clear just from looking at his movements and build that he had grown significantly stronger over the past few months. Whatever his new training regimen was, it must have been an intense one—and dangerous, too, judging by the fresh injuries that seemed to cover his body every time they met.

"Hmph. Just you wait and see. This year's Lindvolus is gonna be interesting, that's for sure," Lester said with a dauntless grin.

At that moment—

"Yo, Lester MacPhail."

"*Ugh…*?! Ms. Yatsuzaki?"

Kyouko, who was Ayato's homeroom teacher again this year, had sneaked up behind Lester, placing a hand on his shoulder.

Lester, having turned suddenly pale, looked around as if searching for some way to escape.

Ignoring his discomfort, Kyouko grabbed him by the neck, pulling him toward herself. "Melissa's pretty worried about you, MacPhail. Getting yourself beat up all the time, and refusing to so much as talk about it. So what's going on? Huh?"

"N-no, it's just…"

"I thought I told you. Melissa's my precious little baby. If you do anything to upset her, I'll make sure it's much worse for you…" Kyouko's eyes bored into him, something close to savagery emanating from inside them.

"Melissa…?" Ayato whispered under his breath.

"Ah, MacPhail's girlfriend," Eishirou murmured back, covering his mouth with his hand.

Now that he mentioned it, Ayato had heard this story from him once before. Lester, it seemed, had found her collapsed in the street due to her chronic illness one day, and so began their budding romance. Ayato had never met her, but apparently, she was a rare beauty and worked at a café in the Rotlicht.

"...How do you know her, Ms. Yatsuzaki?"

"She's one of my old teammates."

"Wha—?!"

That meant she was a member of the only team from Le Wolfe to ever triumph at the Gryps. That, in and of itself, was an extraordinary coincidence.

"So you'd better start talking, MacPhail."

"I can't!"

"Then tell me why you can't!"

"I can't tell you that, either!"

As he tried to dodge her questions, Lester had broken out into a cold sweat, the drops trickling down his forehead. Kyouko, however, was undeterred.

"Yep, peaceful days," Eishirou murmured as he watched on, looking as if he couldn't be happier.

"A secret training program...?" Ayato muttered under his breath.

"Huh? You know something?" Eishirou returned.

"No, it's just that lately, Julis is getting herself injured pretty frequently, too."

Ayato, Julis, and Kirin trained together as often as they could, but they never went so far as to seriously injure one another. Which meant she was no doubt doing something else in her own time.

"Well, both Her Highness and Lester here have their eyes on the Lindvolus. Of course they're gonna want some intensive training. And isn't Her Highness planning to take down Erenshkigal?"

"I guess so..."

What bothered Ayato, though, was how Julis kept finding a way to dodge his questions about whatever it was that she was doing.

Just like Lester was now.

Of course, Ayato trusted Julis not to engage in anything too over-the-top.

Still, there was one thing that had him worried.

When it comes to Orphelia, I don't think she'll be able to restrain herself...

Watching on as Kyouko wrapped her hands around Lester's neck, Ayato decided that he, too, would have to confront Julis more directly about it.

*

"Percival will be taking a leave of absence from us for a while," the student council president of Saint Gallardworth Academy, Elliot Forster, began at the end of the council's usual debriefing session. "As such, her former position in the rankings, number five, is now vacant and will be decided by a special exhibition match. That's all... Ah, Noelle, if you could stay back for a minute?"

"Huh? A-ah, yes..." The green-haired young woman, Noelle Messmer, alias the Witch of Holy Thorns, Perceforêt, cautiously approached from her position by the far wall, her face downturned as the other members of the student council filed past her out of the room.

Elliot tapped his fingers against his desk as he watched them leave. He still wasn't quite able to feel at home in his new position, behind this heavy ebony desk.

Since the retirement of the previous student council president, Ernest Fairclough, following the Gryps, Elliot had inherited three separate roles: He had taken possession of the Runesword, the Lei-Glems; he had reached the top position in the academy's rankings; and he had succeeded the position of student council president.

According to Gallardworth's code, the top-ranked student was automatically named student council president and had full power to appoint all other student council members. Only then was a vote of confidence conducted across the academy to approve the outcome.

That said, it was general practice that all council members would be selected from among the academy's Page Ones. Other students could put their names forward as candidates should the vote of confidence fail to return a majority, but in all of Gallardworth's history, there was no precedent of that ever having actually been necessary.

Elliot had long known that he was in line to succeed Ernest and had been preparing for the role all that time. He was undoubtedly one of the youngest individuals to reach the office, but he was, after all, the heir of the Forster family, one of the primary founders of the foundation known as Elliot-Pound, and had even been selected upon birth to carry the name of his great ancestor. It was a certain fact that he would receive a position at Elliot-Pound upon graduating from Gallardworth, and it was more than likely that sooner or later, he would become the first Genestella to enter the upper management of one of the enterprise foundations that governed the world.

But now that he had finally reached a position of prominence, he couldn't even pass a single day without being keenly reminded of his inadequacy. To begin with, his compatibility rating with the Lei-Glems only barely met the necessary standard at 82 percent, and there was no way that he could confidently say he had a handle on the Orga Lux.

Moreover, he may have defeated Ernest in their official ranking match, but there was no mistaking that Ernest had wanted to yield his position to him in the first place. After all, Ernest's will to fight seemed to have greatly diminished ever since his team's defeat at the Gryps. Elliot doubted he would have been able to defeat him had he transformed into that monster that had shown itself in the championship. While he might have inherited the Lei-Glems, he suspected—as, he assumed, everyone else did—that he would still lose were he to face that side of Ernest. And so, in a way, he had been unable to save face.

And then there were his actual duties as student council president. No matter how you looked at it, there was simply too much to do, and every passing day seemed busier than the last. And with the school fair coming up soon, things were only getting worse.

On top of that, there had been the incident with Percival, and, of course, the current issue with Noelle. He could feel a headache coming on just thinking about it.

"Ah…," he murmured, letting out a tired sigh.

At this, Noelle finally glanced up, her expression one of concern.

Given that her long fringe almost completely covered her eyes, most people would no doubt have had difficulty reading her emotions. Elliot, however, had been close friends with her long enough to understand her feelings.

"E-Elliot? What's wrong?"

"No, I'm okay… And didn't I tell you not to be so familiar in here?" Elliot frowned.

"Ah! S-sorry! I let my guard down, what with everyone else having left…" Despite her words, Noelle seemed somewhat glad.

"Good grief… You can't afford to slip up here."

Elliot and Noelle weren't siblings, but their relationship came close. Ever since the Invertia, the children of the great families of Europe often intermingled at social gatherings and the like. On top of that, the Forster and Messmer families were close in status and in geographical location, and so the two of them had practically been raised in each other's company.

"Anyway, Noelle," Elliot began, clearing his throat. "There's something I want to check with you."

"Oh?"

"Is it true that you've been training with the Ban'yuu Tenra?"

"*Whanya?!*" Noelle stepped backward, letting out a strange moan, before suddenly covering her mouth with her hands and quickly shaking her head from side to side.

"Come on, Noelle. You might as well have just admitted it."

But if this was how she was going to react to his asking, then he wouldn't pry any further.

"B-but how…?"

"Don't underestimate Sinodomius. You might have gotten away with it were it only once or twice, but if you're going to keep going there month after month, they were bound to notice sooner or later. The other schools' intelligence networks have probably picked up on it by now, too."

For her part, the Ban'yuu Tenra herself had no doubt anticipated as much. In any event, he didn't have any proof of her knowing that, but neither was there any particular need for him to divulge that fact.

"Anyway, listen to me, Noelle. Whatever your reasons are, you're being careless and lacking in discretion. This isn't appropriate for one of Gallardworth's Page Ones. And it's out of the question for someone on the student council, let alone someone so close to the president."

"Oh..." Noelle drooped her shoulders despondently.

"That said... The higher-ups are willing to overlook it. Although that does make me a bit uneasy."

"Huh?" Noelle gaped, clearly taken aback by this outcome.

In actual fact, the other schools had taken similar courses of action.

All of them except the Ban'yuu Tenra's own Jie Long, that was.

"If I had to guess, they're probably willing to overlook it precisely because it's the Ban'yuu Tenra. If it were, say, Le Wolfe's Dirk Eberwein, they'd quite reasonably suspect some sort of ulterior motive, but the Ban'yuu Tenra isn't that kind of person. She no doubt just wants to train you—all of you. And besides... If it helps our own students to become stronger, it looks like they regard that as a net win. That said, Jie Long seems to be quite up in arms at their own student council president working with students from rival schools." Elliot stopped there, letting out a deep breath in an attempt to smother his inner thoughts.

What he hadn't told Noelle was that the reaction of the academy's higher-ups was essentially proof that they didn't regard her as being particularly important. That was obviously the *real* deciding factor.

Since becoming the student council president, Elliot had gained access to all kinds of information that had previously been out of his reach—and there was no mistaking that the most shocking among all of that had to do with the Ban'yuu Tenra.

The Ban'yuu Tenra—a battle-crazed monster beyond compare, a being who had inhabited this world for upward of a thousand years.

If she was going out of her way to train students from the other schools, it could only be so that she herself could devour them when she was finished. In other words, no matter how much strength those students managed to obtain, it would still all be for nothing.

It was clear that the losses would outweigh the benefits in the long run. It wasn't the kind of decision that the academy's higher-ups—the enterprise foundation—would normally make.

However, Elliot knew that this time, there was something the foundation was prioritizing over and beyond such normal concerns.

"...Noelle, are you serious about entering the Lindvolus?" he asked, wishing in his heart she would withdraw.

Noelle, however, nodded in confirmation.

There was a tacit understanding among Gallardworth's Page Ones that the top ten of their number would prioritize the team tournament, the Gryps, above all other Festas. While it was, in the end, no more than that—a tacit understanding, with no obligation to comply—Noelle's current stance was nonetheless exceptional.

"But why?! There's no need for you to fight in that freak show! Why do you insist on going it alone? Why can't you wait until the next team tournament?"

It was fair to say that the upcoming Lindvolus would be the most anticipated Festa in decades.

There was every possibility that Orphelia Landlufen could become the first person ever to achieve three consecutive victories in the solo tournament, or that either Ayato Amagiri or Julis-Alexia von Riessfeld would become the second individual to achieve a grand slam. On top of that, Sylvia Lyyneheym had publicly announced her desire to avenge her previous defeat at Orphelia's hands, and rumor had it that one of those automatons from Allekant that had caused such a stir in the Phoenix would be making an appearance, too. There might still be more than six months before the tournament got under way, but it was already a hot topic on the Net and all the television talk shows. The Festa might always have been met with excitement, but this time, things had reached a fever pitch.

That was no doubt why the academy's upper management had decided not to interfere in Noelle's case. They weren't prepared to let Gallardworth, which prided itself on coming out on top in the three-year cycle overall, be overshadowed by any of the other schools.

And so they were willing, this time, to use her as a pawn that they could afford to sacrifice if necessary.

"B-but, I mean… This is the chance I've been waiting for," Noelle murmured in a small voice.

"Chance? What do you mean?"

"To repay you, Elliot."

"Huh…?" Elliot was left speechless by the unexpected response.

Noelle broke into a smile. "You were the one who came to help me, remember, when I was getting bullied as a kid? I've been wanting to do something to thank you for so long, and now I finally have the chance."

So that was it. Noelle certainly wasn't of the strongest character, and back then, she had yet to master her abilities as a Strega. So he had decided to keep an eye out for her. And when she found herself in trouble, he had stepped in to help. That was all there was to it.

"I know how hard it is for you, too, right now, Elliot. It can't be easy following after Ernest Fairclough."

"That's…" Elliot fell silent, forced to acknowledge the truth of what she said.

Ernest had been met with great fanfare since the moment he had first enrolled at Gallardworth, and he soon after secured for himself the number one ranking, mastered the Lei-Glems, and led the academy to victory in the Gryps. He may have finished as a runner-up in his last tournament, but there was no denying that during his time at Gallardworth, he had been at the very top of practically every metric. That was proof not only of his individual fighting ability but also of his impressive tenure as student council president.

Elliot, on the other hand, may have only recently become student council president, but he had already entered the Festa twice, making the top four in the Phoenix and the fifth round in the Gryps. In terms of his own personal contributions to the academy, he couldn't deny that he wasn't up to Ernest's level. That being the case, the only thing for it was to demonstrate his skills and produce results in other areas, but even if he sent the academy's most promising students to the upcoming Lindvolus or the following year's Phoenix—

"!" His thoughts had finally taken him to Noelle's reasoning. "Don't tell me you're planning to…"

"…Yep. I'll do everything I can," she said, clenching her raised fists.

That's not for you to worry about! You don't need to take part!

"!" Elliot managed to swallow the words rising up inside him before they could burst out.

While Noelle was doing it for him, her actions would also benefit the academy. As student council president, he couldn't get in the way of that.

Her actions were born of devotion—a brilliant, radiating virtue.

In other words, they were the kind of action the Lei-Glems was most fond of.

He couldn't put a stop to it. Ernest, perhaps, might have been able to deceive the Orga Lux—but for now, at least, Elliot had yet to find a way of doing so himself.

"…I understand. Thank you, Noelle. We're counting on you." Cursing his powerlessness in the depths of his mind, he could do little but flash her a forced smile as he wrung the words from his lips.

*

Hufeng was in an unusual hurry as he made his way down the corridors of the Hall of the Yellow Dragon.

As the leader of the Wood sect, he wouldn't normally allow himself to appear so flustered. Today, however, was different.

He was making his way to Xinglou, a letter clutched delicately in his hands.

At this time of day, she would no doubt be in the middle of training her disciples in the Room of the Vermilion Bird.

He turned a corner into the corridor surrounding the garden, when—

"Wha—?!"

As he realized that the door that should have been in front of him looked to have been blown off its hinges, he caught sight of a black shadow rolling through the garden with great force.

"Wh-what on earth… Master?!"

As he made sense of the scene in front of him, he realized that it was Xinglou that he was staring at—Xinglou who had been thrown across the garden.

"Heh… Heh-heh-heh! Wonderful! You've exceeded all expectation!" Xinglou's expression was ecstatic as she licked at the blood running across her chin. That could mean only one thing—

Someone had managed to land an attack on her.

But that's… That's…

Hufeng, unable to believe his eyes, froze in place.

There was no one at Jie Long who could do that to Xinglou Fan, the Ban'yuu Tenra. Not even her highest disciple, Xiaohui Wu, had been able to pull off such a feat.

"No, it's all thanks to your training, master. I can't thank you enough."

"Fuyuka…?!"

Stepping out of the Room of the Vermilion Bird was Jie Long's third-ranked student, the Witch of Dharani, Fuyuka Umenokouji.

Her long, lustrous black hair falling over her slender eyes, every movement of her delicate body appeared graceful and composed. Her uniform was that of Jie Long, but her jacket was different, emblazoned with a crest shaped like a Japanese plum.

"I should have expected as much from the Umenokouji clan's hidden techniques. You've surpassed my expectations. Perhaps I'm going to have to get serious." An ominous light glimmered in Xinglou's eyes as an overpowering sense of pressure suddenly erupted from her petite frame, bearing down on Fuyuka.

"No, no, that won't do, master," a remonstrating voice spoke up from behind Fuyuka—the head of the Water sect, Cecily Wong. "You can't mean to crush her before she can take part in the Lindvolus, can you? That would be such a waste."

"Are you trying to get between us, Cecily? It's only thanks to our master's training that I've been able to revive our lost techniques. I'm indebted to her." Despite Xinglou's ominous aura washing over her, Fuyuka's expression had changed only slightly, one eye opening marginally wider. Even so, while her lips were curled upward in a grin, those eyes of hers were unmistakably serious.

"See, she says so herself. There's no harm in a little taste." Xinglou, on the other hand, was already brimming with excitement. As she grumbled under her breath, the air around her began to warp, with three mystical *vajras*, holy weapons, appearing in the empty space before her, circling her like miniature satellites.

Together, the three weapons—the Dokkosho, the Sankosho, and the Gokosho—made up the Gourensho—a *sengu*, or sage tool—left behind by the first Ban'yuu Tenra.

It was Jie Long's greatest treasure, with everyone but Xinglou forbidden to lay so much as a hand on it.

"But I guess if you're going to bring out something like that, then I'll just have to..." Fuyuka, however, continued to maintain her composed demeanor as she quickly set to activating a seal with her fingers.

Hufeng could tell right away that, as a technique, it was completely different to *seisenjutsu*.

"*I beseech thee, oh Taisai, that Ouban's comet may drive out evil, that thou may grant me the protection of the Dragon King of the Sea...*," Fuyuka intoned, a vast vortex of mana building up around her.

This, too, was completely different to Cecily's *seisenjutsu*. At the very least, as far as Hufeng could tell, *seisenjutsu* possessed no technique that consumed as much mana as this.

"H-hold on a minute, you two! Stop! Hufeng, say something to her!" Cecily, letting out an exasperated sigh, stared at him imploringly.

"Ah, well..." Hufeng, still not fully grasping the situation, could do little but continue to stand still in confusion, however.

"Oh, Hufeng? What's that in your hand? Don't tell me it's...," Fuyuka called out, her voice cold and threatening.

This was enough to make him return to his senses. He quickly adopted a formal posture, holding out the letter as he bowed before Xinglou. "Y-yes, master! You've received a message from Senior Disciple!"

"...Oh, have I now?" The sense of intimidation emanating from her immediately vanished. Smiling, Xinglou rushed over to receive the letter.

Fuyuka, watching on from the side, allowed her ability to dissipate with a shrug.

"Let's hope he's doing well..."

After his defeat in their semifinal match at the Gryps, Xinglou's highest disciple and Jie Long's second-ranked fighter, Xiaohui Wu, had taken a leave of absence from Jie Long and embarked on a journey to improve his skills. His goal, of course, was to find his own form of martial arts, and temper it to perfection.

He sought also to change himself, as one who had lived his life so far merely abiding by Xinglou's teachings.

"Hmm, yes... Oh?" Xinglou scanned over the contents of the letter with excitement, until coming to a sudden stop. "He wouldn't... I see... Hah! Ha-ha-ha-ha-ha-ha-ha!" Though she raised her eyebrows in surprise at whatever was written there, she apparently couldn't stop herself from breaking out into a high-pitched laugh. She was laughing so hard, in fact, that tears were beginning to form in the corners of her eyes.

"U-um... Master?"

What on earth could Xiaohui have written?

"I always knew he had a curious destiny, but to think he'd bump into that old fool! He must have been born under one lucky star..."

Xinglou remained unable to control her laughter for a long moment. When she finally regained her composure, she turned her gaze toward Hufeng and the others. "Rest easy. According to this, he's in good health. He'll be busy training now, far away from us all here. And—he should be back for the Lindvolus."

"!" Hufeng startled at this announcement. That meant, no doubt, that he intended to compete.

"Hufeng, I'll trust you to carry out the necessary preparations."

"Of course, master!"

If Xiaohui really was going to enter the tournament, that came as great news for him, too.

Since fighting alongside him in the Gryps, Hufeng had only gained more respect for Xiaohui's strength and earnest nature. And now Xiaohui would take on the Festa once more, and the Lindvolus at that. He felt as if he could finally rest easy.

Hufeng, of course, wished he could compete himself, but having entered two Festas already, he only had one more opportunity remaining. Seeing as he wanted to better himself under Xinglou's guidance a while more yet, he had no choice this time but to give it a miss.

"Hmm… In that case, I might get a chance to fight him myself. Oh, that'll be fun," Fuyuka said, concealing her mirth with the sleeve of her inner kimono. Her unshakable confidence was there for all to see.

To tell the truth, Hufeng had hardly ever seen Fuyuka fight.

While she liked to call herself Xinglou's pupil, she was, strictly speaking, treated by everyone else here as a guest. On top of that, Xinglou had instructed her disciples to refrain from engaging with her as much as possible. She seemed to spend most of her time diligently studying techniques deep within the Hall of the Yellow Dragon.

From what Hufeng had heard, the Umenokouji clan seemed to possess a special bloodline and had passed down a system of techniques not unlike *seisenjutsu* for more than a thousand years. Those techniques were the sole property of the clan, and it seemed to be forbidden to share them with outsiders. Hufeng had gathered that she often engaged with Xinglou, and Cecily, too, being in charge of passing along *seisenjutsu*, but he himself had only had minor dealings with her.

Hufeng had seen her techniques in action only once, during an official ranking match. From what he could tell, the main technique she used then was a unique throwing one, similar to others used in *seisenjutsu* or jujitsu, but that was as much as he was able to learn then. At the time, he had doubted she would be able to stand up to him—let alone someone like Xiaohui.

And yet—

"But you know, Fuyuka, are you really okay with it…? Your techniques, I mean," Cecily asked, her voice tinged with worry.

"What's this now?" Fuyuka replied, tilting her head to one side.

"Well, like… It wouldn't be against the rules, or anything, right?"

"There shouldn't be a problem there…hopefully," Fuyuka said with a loud guffaw.

"At any rate, this year's Lindvolus is getting more and more interesting. One of our friends at the Liangshan even managed to land an attack on me the other day, too."

"Wha—?!" Hufeng, Cecily, and even Fuyuka all startled at this offhand remark.

"By the Liangshan, you mean that private school that you've gone and opened, master? Do you really have anyone that strong there…?"

The private school had become a cause of considerable friction between Xinglou and the executives of integrated enterprise foundation of Jie Long—but at this revelation, Hufeng was willing to put that issue aside for a moment.

"…Who, exactly?" Fuyuka asked the very question that was on the tip of Hufeng's own tongue.

Xinglou, however, responded only with a merry laugh. "Yes, the tournament should be fun, indeed."

*

"And we're done!"

Camilla was working tirelessly in her lab when the door suddenly slid open, her dear friend appearing in the entrance. "—! Ernesta!" she exclaimed when she realized who had spoken earlier.

"Hey, Camilla. Long time no see." Ernesta waved to her with a smile, still yet to properly step inside.

"Where have you been all this time?! I haven't been able to get in touch at all…!"

Ever since the end of the Phoenix, Ernesta had taken to going on frequent, long absences from Allekant—or rather, from Asterisk itself—to the point where Camilla hadn't heard from her in months now. She had, of course, tried to call her friend countless times, but on most occasions, the call simply wouldn't connect, and at those rare moments when it did, Ernesta merely mumbled on and on about equations and the like, as if half-asleep. It had reached a point where Camilla was seriously considering reporting her as missing.

"Sorry, sorry, it was an important time for work I was entrusted with."

"I get that… But it isn't anything shady, is it?"

Camilla herself was often asked to undertake work by outside research institutes, and it wasn't unusual that they could turn into long-term projects. For someone of Ernesta's talents, it was only natural that those requests would be both more numerous and more significant.

That said, it had all gone a bit too far this time.

"Come on, Camilla, you know I'm bound to confidentiality. Well, it was pretty boring work, to be honest, but the generous remuneration more than compensated for all that."

"Remuneration…?" Whatever she must have meant, it probably wasn't money. Given her current sponsors, the number of funds at her disposal was already practically limitless.

"Ah, master! If you had told us you were coming back, we would have prepared a proper reception for you!"

"Welcome back, master."

Ardy and Rimcy both hurried toward them from the depths of the lab.

"You look well, you two. It looks like you're both taking good care of Camilla."

"They've been a great help. Much better than the staff, that's for sure."

Since handing over the leadership of Ferrovius to the next generation, Camilla, though still a student, was in a state of semiretirement (though, of course, she was still busy conducting her own research). The fact that, in spite of that, she had essentially secluded herself in her lab was because she was in the middle of developing a new type of Lux for Rimcy to use in the upcoming Lindvolus.

It was all so she could settle her dispute with Saya Sasamiya once and for all.

That said, having given up the faction's leadership, she could no longer appropriate staff for private purposes. That was why she was having Ardy and Rimcy assist her.

The development of the autonomous puppets was originally a joint project between Ferrovius and Pygmalion, and both groups likewise had joint ownership over them. That meant they weren't Ferrovius's to make sole use of, and so without Ernesta's support, Camilla may very well have found herself working alone, which would have all but quashed her hopes of participating in the Lindvolus.

"...Hmm? Something seems to be happening outside," Camilla murmured as she detected the sound of a frantic voice outside the lab.

They were deep inside Allekant's research facilities, a place where very few people were permitted to enter, so such disturbances were a rare occurrence.

"Is that...a child?"

"Eee-hee-hee! Yep, that's right! There's someone I want to introduce to you! Lenaty! You can come in now!"

"Okaaay!" The cheerful response was instantaneous, followed by the sound of footsteps as the figure ran toward them down the hall.

And then—

"Hiya! What's going on, Mom?" The figure that leaped toward Ernesta, wrapping its arms around her, was that of a small, adorable girl.

"M-M-M...'Mom'?!" Camilla stammered, lost for words at how that spirited child had addressed the woman.

The girl looked to be around ten years old. Her hair was pale blonde in color, and even though it was tied up, it bobbed up and down with her movements. She had a sweet, lovable appearance, with large, round eyes, a small mouth, and soft, plump cheeks—but the most impressive thing about her was an overwhelming sense of innocence.

"E-Ernesta! Wh-when did you...? No, more importantly, who's the...?!" Camilla was left so shaken that she couldn't even finish her sentences.

"Please, calm down, Camilla. She's a puppet," Rimcy explained.

Only then did Camilla recognize her for what she was.

She certainly looked human, as far as her appearance was concerned, but in the depths of those eyes, Camilla could make out the delicate movements of visual sensors, and when she listened carefully, she could vaguely hear faint mechanical noises emanating from inside Lenaty.

"Hey, Mom, hey. Who are these people?" Lenaty asked, tilting her head to the side as she clung to Ernesta's waist.

"All right, listen up," Ernesta began in a tender—well, *coaxing*—tone of voice. "That big guy over there—he's your brother."

"Huh?! My brother?!"

"And that cool lady standing next to him—she's your sister."

"What?! I've got a sister, too?!"

"And this wonderful, tanned beauty is your father."

"Dad!" Lenaty's eyes positively sparkled as she caught Camilla in a tight embrace.

"W-wait a second! I don't remember any of this! And besides, I'm a woman, too! Why am *I* the father?!"

"Eee-hee-hee! Don't worry about the details," Ernesta responded, her voice matter-of-fact.

Camilla ground her teeth in frustration as she looked over Lenaty, who wore a carefree smile as she stared down at her feet.

She was well put together, as expected of something made by Ernesta. Camilla might have been slightly confused at the time, but even she had mistaken her for a real person at first glance.

The problem, however, wasn't her appearance. There were already plenty of puppets that resembled humans to one degree or another. Rather, what had fooled her was the puppet's behavior.

In other words—

"Ernesta, this is a third autonomous puppet." Camilla, her expression turning serious, peered across the room at Ernesta while stroking Lenaty's head.

"That's my Camilla! Meet Autonomous Puppet Prototype LN-T, Lenaty. That's the name I gave her," Ernesta responded nonchalantly as she, too, began to stroke her on the head. "I had my whole lab moved when I took on that other job, but I kept working on her on the side. Oh, I've outdone myself this time."

"...This is the first I've heard about all this," Camilla said in a low voice, trying as best she could to keep her anger from bursting forth as she glared toward Ernesta. "Was this your plan all along?"

Camilla and Ernesta were kindred souls, best friends, and, above everything, collaborative researchers when it came to the autonomous puppets. But in spite of that, Ernesta had gone and created a third such puppet without so much as informing her. If this wasn't betrayal, then what was?

"Mom...?" Perhaps having sensed the tense atmosphere, Lenaty glanced up toward Ernesta uncertainly.

"Lenaty, why don't you go and play with your brother and sister in that room over there?" Ernesta said gently as she stroked her hair.

"Okaaay!"

Camilla motioned toward Ardy and Rimcy to accompany her. The adjoining room was designed for testing Luxes, so there would no problem if they were a bit noisy.

"Bwa-ha-ha! What do you say, my lovely little sister?" Ardy fawned. "Why don't you have some fun with your big brother?"

"Out of the way, you wooden doll! It shall be I, her elder sister, who shall accompany our sweet younger sibling! Now then, child, what would you like to play?" Rimcy doted.

"Battle! Lena wants to battle!"

"I see, I see! In that case, I shall be your partner!" Ardy declared. "Let's see what you can do!"

After watching Rimcy lead Lenaty by the hand into the testing room, Camilla finally turned back to Ernesta.

"…Well, I guess it's only natural that you're upset. But you know, I had to do it by myself. I had to make her alone, without getting you caught up in it." Ernesta's countenance was unusually meek and humble.

"Will you tell me why?"

"So that the responsibility would fall on me if something went wrong."

"What…?" But before Camilla could ask her what she meant, Ernesta pulled out her mobile.

"…Here," she said. "I'm sending you all my data on her."

"Data…?"

Camilla opened several air-windows with her own mobile, scanning over the data, when—

I guess I should have expected as much… The design philosophy is much more advanced than when we built Ardy and Rimcy. And the core…yes, urm-manadite… Wait, there's two of them?! Don't tell me she's using the LOBOS transition method to control them…?!

—she realized that the specs were higher than she could possibly have imagined.

However, the biggest surprise was saved for last. No sooner had her gaze skimmed over the data than she raised a hand to her mouth, staggering backward. "Th-this is…"

"Yes. This is what I've always been striving to accomplish. My ideals. My dream." Ernesta's eyes burned with an almost repellent level of passion. Her avid zeal, at this very moment, was in no way inferior to that of Magnum Opus, Hilda Jane Rowlands.

"Do you… Do you realize what you've done…?"

This was no longer a question of ability or performance.

No, this went much deeper…to the very foundation of what comprised weapons and puppets.

"Of course," Ernesta said, nodding.

At that moment, a terrible boom thundered out from the adjoining testing room.

"Wh-what was that?!" Camilla hurried to open the door, only to find Ardy's giant frame embedded in the wall, Rimcy standing motionless in shock, and, in the center of the room, Lenaty swinging her right arm back and forth exuberantly.

"Lena wins, Lena wins!" The girl-like figure laughed innocently as she hopped across the room.

"Bwa-ha-ha! I've been defeated…!" Ardy sounded like he was all right, but the damage was obvious.

"…Rimcy, what happened?"

"Lenaty broke through his defensive barrier. Empty-handed."

"What…?!" Camilla was left speechless once more. She had lost count of the number of times this new puppet could shock her. "A-anyway, get Ardy to the factory. I'll be along in a minute."

"Understood." Rimcy gathered Ardy up in her arms, taking off toward the factory in the next building over.

"Lenaty. You've overdone it. You're going to have to apologize to your brother for that."

"Huh? But Lena didn't do anything wrong," she protested, puffing out her cheeks.

As she watched Lenaty's reaction, Camilla felt a cold fire begin to burn deep inside her.

This was the exact opposite of everything she believed in. There was no way that she could accept it.

And yet, more important than that—

"…Ernesta, are you planning to have this child take part in the Lindvolus?"

"Yep, of course! You were planning to enter with Rimcy, right? Given how well they performed in the Phoenix, it looks like proxy fighters are going to be allowed again this time."

Camilla let out a deep sigh, steeling her resolve, before glancing back toward Ernesta. "In that case, let me prepare Lenaty's armaments. Given her specs, it wouldn't do to arm her with just any old Lux."

"Huh? That won't do, Camilla! Why would you want to...?" Ernesta shook her head.

Camilla, in an unusual move for her, raised a hand to stop her. "If you're going to have her call me her father, you could at least let me do this much."

"...Don't tell me this is about your body?"

This time, it was Camilla's turn to shake her head.

It was certainly true that Ernesta had built half of Camilla's own body, using the same technology that powered the puppets, and that Camilla, in turn, had sworn to dedicate half of her life to her. And yet—

"That has nothing to do with it. I want this...on a personal level. Intuitively. Some voice deep inside me is telling me I need to do it," Camilla responded, recalling what Hilda had said to her some months prior.

"This seems like a good opportunity to let you in on a little secret. It's that sense of intuition that sets people like me and Ernesta Kühne apart from the likes of you, Camilla Pareto. All great scientists are gifted with intuition. We have it. Mediocre researchers like yourself don't."

If she could see her now, she would throw those words right back at her: *I might not be the best, but I'm a scientist, too, Hilda!*

"...Right. Well, I guess we can do that." Ernesta flashed her a defeated smile.

"Just so you know, I'm still planning on entering with Rimcy as well. If she ends up fighting against Lenaty, I won't let her go easy on her."

She was getting Rimcy ready to be outfitted with a new weapon system designed specifically to defeat Saya Sasamiya.

With that, she ought to at least be a match for Lenaty. It would leave Ardy at a disadvantage, but that couldn't be helped this time around.

"Oh? I'd expect nothing less." Ernesta's laugh was just like Lenaty's, as if they really were mother and child.

*

"Ha-ha-ha-ha! 'Sup, ladies! Aren't we as beautiful as ever! Why don't you give us a hug, eh?"

Irene was passing her lunch break at the Le Wolfe Black Institute the same way she always did—sitting at a picnic table with her sister, Priscilla, in the courtyard in front of the main school building, gulping down a lunch her sister had made—when a man with sunglasses, standing at the head of a crowd of close to twenty people, suddenly called out to her.

He was tall and burly; his chest was covered in a layer of thick red hair; and his teeth glinted as he shone her a broad and somewhat threatening smile. His eyes may have been hidden behind his sunglasses, but it was quite clear that he was in a cheerful mood. His arms and neck—practically his whole uniform, for that matter—sparkled with all kinds of luxury accessories.

"*Tch!* What do you want, Rodolfo? Don't come any closer…!" Irene warned, rising to her feet and spearing the man with a threatening glare. This was the Institute's second-highest-ranked fighter, Rodolfo Zoppo—the Mage of the Crushing Star, alias Basadone.

"Irene…," her sister tried.

"Keep your distance, Priscilla."

Priscilla fell back as instructed. Compared with how she had been even less than a year ago, her movements now displayed no openings or weaknesses. Her training with the Ban'yuu Tenra must have been paying off, but it still wouldn't be a good idea for her to get involved with the man in front of them. It was always a bad turn of events to get caught in his line of sight.

"Hey, hey, hey! Come on now, I didn't do nothing! We're just here to have some fun, right? Ha-ha-ha!" Rodolfo spread his arms wide, letting out a gregarious laugh. That sentence—*We're just here to have some fun*—was practically his catchphrase.

"Unfortunately, we've got no plans to hang out with you or your thugs," Irene reiterated. "We're having lunch, so scram."

"Come on now," Rodolfo continued, completely ignoring her demonstrations. "You know, I heard a little rumor. That you and your sis are gonna enter the Lindvolus. Is it true?"

"...So what if it is?"

Rodolfo was the head of the Omo Nero, the largest mafia organization operating out of the Rotlicht. It was said that the group had over a thousand members, and that much of the Le Wolfe Black Institute was under their control. Their ability to gather information wasn't to be underestimated.

"So it's true, then? Well, damn it. So you think you can take down Erenshkigal? You'd be better off rethinking that. There ain't anything fun about that kinda work. Don't you think?"

"I'm afraid that, unlike you, we're not looking to have fun."

Rodolfo's point wasn't, however, entirely incorrect.

There was no debating that Orphelia Landlufen was the indisputable favorite to win, but the other schools were all entering formidable contestants, too. Irene's job, as Dirk had instructed her, was to take down as many of them as possible.

Not only that, but this time, she would receive a bonus for every opponent she defeated. In other words, the better she performed, the closer she could come to clearing her debt. Just thinking about it was enough to get her worked up.

"Hah! What a sad way to go! Why don't you quit whoring yourself out and come have some fun at our place? Come on, we'll take care of your money problems. I'll even give you a loan!"

"Who are you calling a whore?! I'll kill you if you so much as try to lay one of those fat, disgusting fingers of yours on either of us!"

The Omo Nero wasn't exactly hostile to Dirk, but they weren't exactly on good terms, either.

"...Hey, asshole. What makes you think you can talk to the boss like that?" a burly skinhead bellowed, stepping forward from the crowd. Irene didn't remember his name, but she remembered seeing his face amid the rookies who had recently entered the school's rankings. "I don't care if you're third or not, if you disrespect the boss—"

"Heeey! We're just inviting these beauties to have a bit of fun! You gonna get in the way? Huh?" Rodolfo, still wearing his artificial smile, glared at the man with the full strength of the midsummer sun.

"Gwuh...?!"

At that moment, the skinhead's skull seemed to burst into flames.

He fell limp, the whites of his eyes showing as he lay sprawled faceup on the ground. Fortunately, it looked like he was still breathing. His head seemed badly burned on the left side, but it was still intact, at least.

Without even glancing toward him, Rodolfo made a sign with his fingers, and some of his other followers began to drag the skinhead away.

"...Damn it, this ain't fun. But remember this. You and your sister are both my type. So I don't wanna have to hurt you."

"Huh? What's that supposed to mean?"

"Ha-ha-ha! I'm gonna be in it, too! The Lindvolus!"

"!"

Rodolfo was currently in his second year of college but, until now, hadn't even entered the Festa once.

Irene, like practically everyone else, had assumed he simply wasn't interested in it.

"Oh? What's gotten into you? You've left it a bit late, don't you think?"

"Huh? It'll be fun! Ha-ha-ha!" Rodolfo bellowed with laughter once more, before turning his back to her. "Go easy on me if we bump into each other there, won't ya?" And with that, he disappeared into his crowd of followers.

"...Hmph." Only after watching him disappear behind the school building did Irene allow herself to relax.

"Sis, are you okay...? Have some water."

"Ah, that was tense..." She took a mouthful from the bottle that

Priscilla had offered her. "*Brrg!* That bastard! Does he think his rank gives him the right to act that way or something?"

"Um, I was watching the whole time, and he didn't leave any openings or anything..."

"Oh? So you can tell that now, can you?"

Priscilla's growth over the past few months certainly was remarkable. As a regenerative, she had a lot of hidden potential, and if she kept on following her current path, there was every possibility that she could undergo a dramatic transformation from her prior self. She still wasn't strong enough, however, to face Rodolfo or his lackeys.

"...If you wind up facing him in the Lindvolus, tell me you'll withdraw."

Among the Genestella, Rodolfo's ability made him close to invincible.

The only real exception to that was Orphelia. In fact, Rodolfo had challenged her only once and been soundly defeated. But if he had been able to get within range of her, Irene couldn't help but wonder what the outcome would have been.

"Sorry, Irene. I won't withdraw, not even then."

"Huh...?" Irene stared back at her younger sister in mute shock.

"I mean, I'm the best one to face him, right? In terms of tactics and ability. With that battle style of yours, you're the one we should be worried about."

"W-well, that might be true, but..."

At the moment, Irene's fighting style revolved around close combat. No matter how she tried to look at it, she clearly wasn't suited to face Rodolfo.

"You remember what I told you, right? That if you're going to fight, I'll fight alongside you," Priscilla said earnestly, leaning forward. "We'd better finish eating. Break's almost over!" she continued with a gentle smile, holding out the lunch box.

"...I'm no match for you, huh?" Irene could do nothing but return her sister's grin before lifting a stick of skewered meatballs to her mouth.

*

The air-window still open, Sylvia, dressed only in her underwear, held out a one-piece dress in front of the mirror.

"Hmm, I guess this one's a little… Hmm…"

It was certainly pretty, but the design was perhaps a little girly. She wanted to convey a slightly classier impression.

Her bed was covered in a huge pile of clothes that she had taken out of her wardrobe.

"And—are you even listening to me, Sylvia?" Petra's exasperated voice came from the other side of the air-window.

"No. You keep saying the same thing over and over again, Petra."

At this honest response, Petra's expression became suddenly sullen. Sylvia could imagine her eyes, though hidden behind her visor, staring up at her. *"I'm only thinking about what's best for you…"*

"Ha-ha! Come on, Petra, you don't expect me to believe that after all we've been through?"

"…Taking your achievements and abilities into account, it only makes sense to give the upcoming Festa a miss," she continued in a soft voice. *"If you wait till the next Lindvolus, your chances of winning will be considerably greater."*

In other words, Petra thought she wouldn't be able to defeat Orphelia and was urging her not to waste her limited opportunities to enter the tournament.

Despite this, Sylvia didn't feel insulted by the older woman's appraisal. No matter how you looked at it, Orphelia's power was undeniably overwhelming.

"I understand the logic behind what you're saying, but why are you only bringing it up now? Before, you were happy not to interfere with whatever I decided to do, whether to enter or not. Isn't that right, Petra?"

"The situation has changed. It would be one thing if we could be certain that you would reach Orphelia in the final, but I fear that such a view is now rather optimistic."

"I see. So you'd be happy if I could make runner-up. Still, the answer is no. I've already publicly declared my intent to take revenge on Orphelia, so if I drop out now, everyone will think I'm too cowardly to follow through."

As she spoke, she thought of perhaps adopting a monochrome look, with black skinny pants and a white shirt, but she soon changed her mind. That would be too simple. She really was in a bind here.

"Which is why I'm suggesting we organize a large-scale live tour to take place over the winter. If you're clearly busy with work, that should lessen the criticism."

That was half-true—and half-wrong.

Sylvia's popularity came not only from her musical career but also because that career had been born out of her performance in the arena. If she were to turn her back on all that, the mainstay of her fan base would collapse beneath her.

"As I told you before, there are too many irregularities with this year's Lindvolus. Orphelia Landlufen is just the tip of the iceberg. Every school is entering their best fighters this time around. Everyone, except perhaps Gallardworth's entrants, will pose a considerable challenge. There's no guarantee that you'll be able to reach the championship."

"Isn't that a good thing, if my opponents are stronger? It'll certainly get the crowd more excited. And that'll work to my advantage too, no?"

On top of that, she fully intended to carry out her responsibilities as Queenvale's reigning top-ranked fighter.

"Neithnefer will compete even if you don't. On top of that, Violet Weinberg's growth has been extraordinary, as has Minato Wakamiya's… Although I suppose we have the Ban'yuu Tenra to thank for those two."

"Ah, speaking of Minato, has she gotten that Orga Lux yet?"

Sylvia hadn't seen her for a while now but hoped she was managing to keep well.

When she thought of that puppy-like—no, rabbit-like—girl she always felt her lips forming a smile. Minato just had a certain charming aura about her.

"We also have—"

"Yes, yes, I know. I *am* the student council president, you realize?"

"Then, will you withdraw?"

"Those are separate issues."

"...Sylvia." Petra's voice seemed to drop down a level.

Perhaps she had finally managed to anger her, Sylvia wondered.

"Hmm, well, it isn't that I don't trust everyone. But you know, I don't intend to lose. No matter who my opponent is."

Even if she faced Ayato, the champion of both the Phoenix and the Gryps, for example, she would still be confident in her victory.

But it sounded like he wasn't going to enter out of consideration for Julis.

Just thinking about how dearly he seemed to regard that princess with the rose-colored hair was enough to make her feel slightly...no, pretty jealous.

"Words alone won't secure victory. What makes you so sure?"

"I'm preparing some new songs. Three, in fact... I wrote one of them for Orphelia especially."

"Three...? Why am I only hearing about this now?"

Sylvia used her songs to activate her abilities and so took sole responsibility for composing both the arrangements and the lyrics. For that reason, when she wanted to manifest a particular effect, they often required considerable time and effort to produce (she could still improvise, of course, but in that case, their accuracy and strength would be greatly reduced).

"They're not finished, that's why. I was going to tell you when they were ready."

"Hmm..." Petra sank deep into thought, no doubt realizing that the conditions had changed yet again.

"Sorry, Petra. I know why you're telling me to quit, and I can see your logic, but I want to do this. And I want to win, against Orphelia."

She still wasn't able to forget the depths of her regret that day she had lost in the championship match of the last Lindvolus.

"I can't give this up."

She was, after all, a sore loser.

All the targets that she had set for herself—as a songstress, as Queenvale's top-ranked fighter, in her search for Ursula, and in the pursuit of love—she wanted to succeed in every one of them. She was fighting to achieve all of those goals.

Of course, there were things that she simply wouldn't be able to do. As frustrating as it was, there would be times when she'd be forced to accept setbacks, when she would have to decide between one thing or another. But at the very least, she didn't want to have to live with regrets when such times came.

"Well... All right. If you're that set on it, I guess there's no talking you out of it." With this, Petra let out a deep sigh, her shoulders slumping. She looked to have finally given up. *"Why don't you try the off-shoulder blouse at the end of the bed, along with those culottes in front of you?"*

"Huh?"

"You're going on a date with Ayato Amagiri, no?"

"Ah... Well, something like that."

Strictly speaking, it wasn't a date, but rather, one of their regular meetings to exchange information on the Golden Bough Alliance. That, however, didn't mean she still wasn't going to give it her all. She didn't get many opportunities to meet Ayato in person, and she had her heart set on winning the contest over him.

"Oh, this *is* nice..."

As she lifted the two pieces that Petra had suggested in front of her, she could only nod in satisfaction at the refreshing look.

"Nice advice. There's no beating a former top idol and model," Sylvia said in praise.

Petra relaxed her mouth into a faint smile. *"Given your attitude toward losing, I have to support you where I can. Although, if you were to ask me, I would warn you that your opponents are quite formidable... Do your best.*" With that, the air-window snapped shut before Sylvia could even determine whether she was trying to be sarcastic or encouraging.

"...I don't need you to tell me that, Petra."

But, of course, she was right.

In a sense, her current contest was even more grueling than the Lindvolus.

CHAPTER 6
PRELUDE

"Heeey, Ayato!"

The first day of the school fair was met with refreshing, clear weather. Beneath that cloudless sky, the plaza in front of the Sirius Dome was bustling with people, but fortunately, Ayato had no difficulty spotting his beaming, waving sister.

Not wanting to stand out too much, he had partially disguised his appearance with a pair of fake glasses and a cap, as he usually did when he went out in public these days. Haruka, however, evidently had no difficulty recognizing him.

"I knew it'd be busy, but this is something else. Maybe we should have picked a different place?" she commented.

"Everywhere's like this during the school fair. Anyway, how's Dad?" Ayato asked.

Haruka had returned to their father's place in Shinshu for a month, only having come back to Asterisk the previous day.

Even after she had been discharged from the hospital, the city guard still had some questions and so forth that they wanted to get out of the way. When, finally, she was free to do as she wished, she took the first opportunity available to return home to see their father, Masatsugu.

"Yep, he's good. He's still as stubborn and sulky as ever...and to be honest, I think he's got a few more gray hairs."

"Ha-ha-ha... I suppose we've both given him enough to worry about. You should have stayed for longer, though, after going all that way."

Although it might not have felt as if much time had passed for Haruka since she had last seen her father, to him, it had been their first reunion in ages. It wasn't hard to imagine that he had, no doubt, wanted to spend more time with her.

"I wanted to, but there's so much to do. She was trying not to be pushy, but Helga wanted me to come back soon, too, so I really couldn't afford to stay there too long."

The city guard might have finished questioning her and, indeed, sealed the case from public knowledge, but there was still every likelihood that Lamina Mortis had his sights on her.

Given their past relationship, there was little doubting that Lamina Mortis was considerably attached to her. While he might have been reluctant to make another move against her life, he could try to recruit her once more. Helga's real reason for wanting her to stay in Asterisk was no doubt to keep her close in order to protect her.

Stjarnagarm, however, didn't have the resources to dispatch officers to watch over her twenty-four seven while, at the same time, conducting an investigation in pursuit of a number of unknown, unnamed individuals. As a compromise, they had therefore agreed to enlist her, at least temporarily, to assist in their efforts.

For that reason, just in case anything was to go wrong, they had given her a tracking device to keep tabs on her whereabouts.

"Besides, I wanted to see the school fair myself, at least once," she said with a faint smile as she watched the crowds with longing eyes.

"...I see."

"On that note, why don't you show me around today?" Haruka said, clapping him on the shoulder.

"Right, leave it to me."

As it happened, Ayato had been shown around each of Asterisk's six schools last year by Sylvia and so would have no trouble guiding Haruka this time around.

At that moment, he suddenly realized something that he had only been subconsciously aware of.

Right... Sylvia's a lot like Haruka. Her mood, the way she acts...

Of course, their builds and facial features were completely different. And while there were a lot of similarities in their personalities, there were plenty of differences, too. But their presences, and their ways of speaking, were, at times, remarkably alike.

Perhaps that was why, he reflected, he had been able to become such fast friends with the world's most popular songstress.

"It makes sense to check out every corner of the city, seeing as I'm planning to join the city guard. It sounds like they can't just walk into the school grounds, either, so this will be a good opportunity."

"About that, Haruka... Are you really serious about it?" Ayato asked as they began to make their way toward the nearby subway station.

"Of course. Lamina Mortis is still working behind the scenes around here somewhere, and I'd like to repay everyone for looking out for me all this time. This way, I can kill two birds with one stone, right?"

"I guess that's true..."

Speaking for himself, however, Ayato couldn't say he approved of her decision.

After all, he had only just been able to safely reunite with her, and now she was preparing to leap once more into harm's way.

"Well, technically, they don't let people involved in an investigation join in on it, so I'll just be doing whatever Helga asks me to."

"...That's a shame."

Given that Stjarnagarm seemed to be perennially understaffed (they had even attempted to recruit Ayato at one point), someone with Haruka's skills and abilities would undoubtedly be of great help to them.

"All I have to do now is pass the recruitment exam."

"That's coming up soon, right?"

"Yep. So I had to keep studying even when I went home."

The fact that she was still being made to sit the recruitment exam only served to prove how serious Helga was about those she enlisted.

The real reason the city guard was so understaffed was that most applicants failed to pass the recruitment process, either at the interview stage or the exam. Only those personally recognized as being of exceptional caliber by Helga were permitted to don the uniform of Stjarnagarm.

"Hold on a second," Ayato murmured as his mobile started ringing.

He pulled it from his pocket, checking the name on the display, when—

"...Magnum Opus!" His brow curled in suspicion, but he nonetheless moved into a shaded area by a nearby building and opened an air-window.

"Kee-hee-hee-hee! Long time no see, Ayato Amagiri! How has your sister been since we woke her?"

"I'm doing fine, thanks to you," Haruka answered, pushing herself into the frame of the air-window. "Hilda, was it? Thanks for taking care of me back then," she said, bowing her head.

Regardless of the circumstances or her motivations for doing so, it *was* Hilda who had successfully woken her, so it was only reasonable to thank her.

"Oh, so you're together now? Well, in any case, you fulfilled your end of the bargain, so there's no need to stand on ceremony."

Ayato doubted that Hilda was trying to be humble by saying that—she no doubt truly believed it. Judging by her way of speaking, she didn't seem particularly interested in Haruka anymore.

"So what do you want?"

"Yes, let's get straight to the point. We're getting ready to resume our experiments with the mana accelerator, so I'm letting you know in advance, as promised."

What she meant, no doubt, was human experimentation.

"I assume the subject gave their full and informed consent and understands all the risks involved?"

"Kee-hee-hee-hee! Of course! They understand it completely, perfectly, without any room for doubt!"

"...Can you prove that?"

"Indeed, indeed! Of course I can! Only too easily! After all—the subject is me*!"*

Ayato was left speechless. "Wha—?!"

He had never suspected that she might subject herself to her own experiments.

Her passion for that research of hers seemed to have descended into total madness.

"How about it? I trust you don't have any objections? Kee-hee-hee-hee! In that case, until next time!" Hilda cut off the transmission with a laugh.

Ayato couldn't say he was particularly happy with this turn of events, but it was true that he had no right to protest.

But even so, he had a bad feeling about it.

He couldn't exactly pin that feeling down, but he knew enough about her research to know it spelled misfortune much more than it did progress.

And if something were to happen in the course of it, there was no questioning the fact that he, too, would bear part of that responsibility.

"...Ayato." Haruka peered at him, her expression looking somehow apologetic.

"Sorry. I guess I'm shouldering a lot of responsibilities right now."

"...That isn't for you to worry about, Ayato."

Right. No matter what happened, he couldn't regret the decisions that had brought his sister back to him.

"Ah, look! If we don't hurry, we won't be able to make it to all of the schools. You wanted to go to Gallardworth first, right?" Ayato said, taking her by the hand and plunging once more into the crowd.

She startled for a brief second, before tightening her grip on his hand, too. "...You really have grown," she murmured, an indecipherable smile tinged with both happiness and regret rising to her lips.

*

The school fair at Saint Gallardworth Academy reflected the formality and social rules of the school's traditions.

There were few stalls or stands around the grounds. In their place, areas such as the cafeteria had been especially set aside for the event, and other buildings were specifically set up to provide spaces for balls, theater productions, concerts, and other social and cultural gatherings.

"Ooh...impressive," Haruka cooed with admiration as she surveyed the central square. "I can see why they call this place Asterisk's most prestigious school."

Ayato, who had had the same reaction last year, found himself grinning.

The buildings were all designed to imitate early modern European architecture, and so, along with Jie Long's Asian style, was among the most visually unique places in Asterisk.

"Well... This is a surprise," a voice came from behind Ayato's back.

"Ernest!" he exclaimed, turning around.

"The last time we saw each other was at the Gryps, if I'm not mistaken. You look well, Ayato." The blond youth shone Ayato a dazzling smile. "Although, I have to say, your disguise is somewhat lacking," he added, resting his chin in one hand as he looked him over.

"Sylvia said the same thing last year," Ayato said with a laugh. "I'm surprised you can make your way through these crowds in one piece."

Ayato was well aware of Ernest's popularity.

"Come now, I think you'll find that so long as you don't draw attention to yourself, you'll be fine."

Indeed, as Ernest said, while there were many people around them who stopped what they were doing when they noticed him, none of them called out to him directly. Perhaps that was thanks to his aura of confidence.

"...Ernest, I'm going to buy something to drink."

"Ah. Thanks, Diana."

The woman who had spoken to Ernest gave Ayato and Haruka a slight bow in greeting before disappearing into the crowd. She looked to be around the same age as Ernest—a beauty with a neat and tidy appearance and a composed, short-cut hairstyle.

"Ernest, is that...?"

"...Yes, my childhood friend."

That was the full extent of Ernest's response, but Ayato could tell from their brief exchange that they were more than that.

"And this fine lady, I assume, is your sister?"

"Pleased to meet you, Ernest. I'm Haruka Amagiri," she said with a quick bow. "The championship match of the Gryps was amazing. The best part was when you cast the Lei-Glems aside toward the end."

"Ha-ha, that wasn't a particularly praiseworthy moment, I'm afraid. My technique was rather unseemly..."

"Not at all, it was much more interesting than your usual overly delicate style."

Ernest blinked in surprise at these comments, as if caught unawares.

"It's important to keep your savagery under control, but it also serves as the foundation for a good technique," Haruka went on. "From what I saw, I think you've got the potential to become a wonderful sword master."

"...I think this is the first time anyone's ever said something quite like that to me," Ernest said with a bright smile much younger than his years. "So this is your teacher, Ayato? I can see why you're so strong."

"Yes, I'm very proud of her," Ayato said, somewhat embarrassed.

"Well then, I should be going..." Ernest gave him a wry smile before turning to leave. "Ah, yes, Ayato," he added with a meaningful glance over his shoulder. "You seem to have quite a bit on your mind. I'm no longer the student council president here, but as it happens, that gives me quite a bit more flexibility than I had before. So if you ever need anything, feel free to ask. I might not be capable of much, but I'll help you out where I can."

"...Thank you."

The night before their championship match at the Gryps, Ernest had come to Ayato's defense when he had been attacked by Lamina Mortis. Perhaps he was referring to that incident, Ayato wondered. But then again, as the former student council president, perhaps he possessed deeper knowledge than he let on. Gallardworth's clandestine operations organization, Sinodomius, was renowned for their intelligence-gathering abilities, after all.

"He seems like a nice person," Haruka remarked.

"Yeah. He used to be the student council president here. It's pretty impressive that he can still act so noble despite having let go of the Lei-Glems."

Among fans of the Festa, his status as the fifth generation in a line of master swordsmen was no empty title.

"Right," Haruka said reproachfully as she put her hands on her hips. "The one who drew the least attention in that match was you, the wielder of the Ser Veresta. You still can't properly control your prana, huh?"

"Ugh..." Ayato had no defense against that criticism.

"Well, if it's a problem with your senses, practice alone won't cut it. And I get that it's more difficult for you given your high level of prana, but still... That's it, come see me when you've got time, and I'll show you a thing or two."

"All right. I've been trying to fix it by myself, but as you can see..."

"Then it's decided."

And with that, the two of them moved on to their next destination.

Even at night, the commercial area during the school fair could hardly be rowdier, with the excitement of day carrying on long past the setting of the sun. Even small avenues two or three streets away from the main boulevard were still crowded with students and tourists alike who were making their way from one place to another.

"Ah, that was awesome!" Haruka exclaimed as she stretched both arms into the air.

"We only managed to make it to Gallardworth, Le Wolfe, and Allekant, though," Ayato remarked.

That said, even going to those three in one day was quite a feat.

"If you're free tomorrow, why don't we check out the others, too?" he added. "We might even bump into Yuzuhi at Queenvale."

"Ah, I almost forgot. Yeah, I'd better say hi to her sometime."

Yuzuhi Renjouji, a member of Queenvale Academy for Young Ladies' Team Kaguya, which had been widely viewed as a dark horse team at the previous Gryps, had long studied archery at one of the Amagiri Shinmei style's branch schools and was a longtime friend to both Ayato and Haruka alike.

"But I'm fine, really. I can find my own way. It wouldn't be fair to the others for me to monopolize you for the whole school fair." Haruka, a step ahead of him, laughed over her shoulder.

By *the others*, she was probably talking about everyone in Team Enfield.

"I don't really have anything planned..."

And for that matter, his four team members all seemed to be busy doing their own things.

It might have been more than half a year away, but Julis was still training nonstop for the Lindvolus.

Saya had practically shut herself away in her new development facilities in the harbor block ever since it opened at the beginning of the school year. She seemed to be perennially busy working on some kind of new Lux with her father, Souichi, and a handful of junior researchers.

Claudia, for her part, was still swamped with work as Seidoukan's student council president—but on top of that, she was deeply involved in their investigation into the Golden Bough Alliance, too, and so had even less free time than usual.

And Kirin, ever since visiting her family at the beginning of the year, had been concentrating on basic training practically nonstop.

"You know, you could try paying a bit more attention to them all."

"Huh?"

"Did you even tell them about coming here with me?"

"I did bring it up during lunch once, I think," Ayato said, retracing his memories.

Haruka narrowed her eyes, glaring back at him. "Good grief... Huh?" Before she could say anything more, she came to a sudden stop.

"What is it, Haruka?" But at that moment, he felt it, too.

Without him having realized it, the scenery around them had undergone a complete change. Where before the streets had been lined with more shops and restaurants than he could count, now they were surrounded by crumbling, abandoned buildings, and a desolate, deserted main street. They were in the redevelopment area.

They might have been taking a short detour, but they should still have been heading toward the station.

"I've sensed this feeling before. Right before that spat with Yabuki..."

Just as now, back then he had found himself winding up in the redevelopment area completely unawares.

At that time, Eishirou had used a secret concealment technique to interfere with his sense of direction.

Not again...

But then, in defiance of his expectations, a woman wearing what looked like a mechanical necklace stepped near them from behind a ruined building.

"...Varda-Vaos!" Ayato shouted. He and Haruka both readied themselves, backing away from the approaching figure. "How are you able to use the Night Emit's techniques...?"

"My strengths lie in mental interference. Now that I know how it works, recreating the same effect is trivial," she replied flatly.

"I see, so you're the Varda-Vaos," Haruka called out. "I suppose we should greet each other properly?"

"Indeed, this is our first time meeting in person. I was working behind the scenes back when we last had reason to encounter each other, in a different body."

But considering she was the only one who could have planted those fake recollections in Haruka's memory, there was no doubting they must have come into direct contact at least once. Perhaps that was after Haruka had already placed her seal on herself, Ayato wondered.

"What do you want with us?" Ayato asked as he carefully scanned his surroundings.

Based on past experience, it was probably—

"I'm the one who wanted to see you. It's been a while, Ayato Amagiri."

—just as he had suspected:

The figure emerging from the shadows behind Varda was none other than Lamina Mortis.

"And…it really has been a long time. You look well, Haruka."

"…"

In stark contrast to Mortis's faint grin, Haruka's expression could hardly be sterner.

"Heh-heh, you're a cold one, daughter mine. Well, never mind. I don't have a lot of time, so let me get straight to the point." He paused as he shifted his gaze. "I would very much appreciate it if you would enter the Lindvolus, Ayato."

"What…?" Ayato broke into a deep frown.

Mortis, however, paid that little heed. "From what I hear, you're trying to avoid entering. That would be such a waste. Now that you've finally broken free of the seal that your sister placed on you, you could become one of the greatest fighters in all of the Festa's history. I would very much like for you to demonstrate that power to the world."

"…Why is that so important to you?"

"No one has ever secured both three consecutive wins and a grand slam in the Festa," Lamina Mortis continued, completely ignoring his question. "And there will probably never be another chance

again. You are a living miracle, Ayato. It's no exaggeration to say that this promises to be the most exciting Festa in history… So let me say it once more!" he proclaimed, raising his arms into the air dramatically. "You must enter the Lindvolus!"

"That's easy for you to say!" Ayato ground out. "But I'm not about to get in Julis's way!"

"Ah, you misunderstand." Mortis shook his head. "This isn't a request. Think of it as…a threat." And with that, an Orga Lux appeared in his hand, the Raksha-Nada activating in front of him.

"!"

Ayato immediately reached for the Ser Veresta, with Haruka activating her own blade-type Lux not a second later.

No sooner had she adopted a defensive stance, however, than her face writhed in agony, and she raised a hand to her chest.

"Ngh…!"

"Haruka!"

It was the same kind of reaction that she had had while talking to him at the hospital. By the looks of it, she still wasn't fully recovered.

"I'm okay, Ayato. We've got bigger things to worry about…!" she declared as she got her breathing under control, fixing Lamina Mortis with a deadly glower.

Ayato was worried about her condition, but she was right. They needed to find a way out of their present situation before they could think about anything else.

"There's no need to push yourself if your body still isn't up to it, Haruka." Mortis fixed Ayato with a placid grin before stabbing the Raksha-Nada into the ground.

"You don't need to worry about me…," Haruka said to her brother before turning to their assailant and beginning to focus her energy. "In the end, all you've got going for you is brute force, huh? But if that's how you want to do it, I'm happy to oblige!"

Ayato, following her lead, lowered his body, raising the Ser Veresta up to eye level. "That's right. We've got reason enough to fight you."

Lamina Mortis was strong. Having crossed swords with him once before, Ayato had tasted the depths of his power. But unlike their last encounter, he was now free from the seal that had been placed on him—and moreover, Haruka was standing alongside him. He didn't intend to lose.

"Heh, brute force, you say? There's nothing wrong with that," Lamina Mortis said, concentrating his own prana in turn.

And then—

Several magic circles appeared around the man, each linked to normally invisible chains stretching all the way to his body. There was no mistaking them: They were exactly the same as the seal that had bound Ayato—in other words, Haruka had sealed away his power, too.

Now that he thought about it, Haruka had indeed said something along those lines: that when she fought him in the Eclipse, even though she lost, she had managed to seal away her opponent's strength.

In that case, the person that Ayato fought last time had been—

"...Well then," Lamina Mortis said calmly with a wave of his left hand. With that gesture, the chains that had been holding him burst into an explosion of light—before disappearing entirely.

He had broken through the seal by force—just as Ayato often had with his own.

And as he did so, something dreadful welled up from inside Lamina Mortis.

"Hmm... It's been a while since I've called on my full power like this," he said as he let out a deep sigh, his voice filled with emotion.

But, of course, if Ayato had been able to break through his seal, it only made sense that Lamina Mortis could do the same with his own. And similarly, if he didn't release the restraints properly, he would no doubt be bound by a time limit and would suffer the side effects when that limit ran out.

And yet—

"Wh-what...?!"

"...Don't let him get to you, Ayato," Haruka said, her face grim as sweat began to gather on her brow.

Without having even realized it, Ayato had found himself

overcome by an instinctive fear, not unlike what he had experienced when encountering Erenshkigal or the Ban'yuu Tenra. Helga had called both of them different and said they existed on a whole other plane.

The same, it seemed, could be said about the man standing in front of them.

If, that was, one took out that overwhelming aura of savagery, that ominous sense that he could devour anything, and then spit them out crushed.

"Now, then! Show me the power that runs through your blood once more!" Lamina Mortis yelled, his voice ringing out as he rushed toward them.

"Ngh!"

Ayato managed to parry the Raksha-Nada with the Ser Veresta, but the force of the blow was enough to send him stumbling backward.

It's too heavy...!

Given that his opponent had swung the Raksha-Nada with only one hand, Ayato could only imagine what would have happened if he had put his whole body into it.

Lamina Mortis's speed and strength were at a completely different level than their last encounter.

"Argh!"

There was a flash of light as Lamina Mortis followed through with a strike aimed at Haruka's torso, but then he made a completely unexpected move, grabbing hold of her barehanded and hurling her backward.

Ayato took advantage of that opening to pull away from their opponent and regain his footing at a distance, only giving Haruka a fleeting glance to check that she had landed safely.

"Amagiri Shinmei Style, Hidden Technique—"

With Lamina Mortis caught between the two of them, Ayato and Haruka synchronized their breathing before unleashing a simultaneous attack.

"*—Crescent Carnage!*"

But just before their strikes could reach him, Mortis seemed to shimmer in the air like a hot flame.

"Ha-ha! Looks like you're still wet behind the ears!"

Their opponent hadn't even broken a sweat.

The Crescent Carnage essentially involved cutting down one's opponent as one ran past them, but Lamina Mortis had managed to send them both flying with one wave of the Raksha-Nada.

"How about this?" he cried out, unleashing a chain of consecutive attacks, each one unbelievably heavy, enough to almost send the Ser Veresta flying from Ayato's hands.

It took everything Ayato had just to hold his ground.

"Looks like you've still got a long way to go! What's the use in talking if you can't even handle the Ser Veresta?"

"What gives you the right to say that?!" Ayato, his anger seething, moved to counter—realizing only too late the mistake that he had just made.

Now that he was within range, Lamina Mortis shifted his body, thrusting him out of the way as he made a strike at Haruka, who tried to attack him from behind.

"Guh...!"

She managed to parry his blade at the last moment, but the difference in their respective abilities was obvious. Haruka, no doubt realizing that for herself, leaped backward to put some distance between them at the first opportunity.

Ayato fought to get himself under control, regaining his fighting stance and glaring balefully at Lamina Mortis.

There was no form to his opponent's swordsmanship. His stance, his movements, his timing were all unique, offense and defense flowing together with a flawless rhythm that Ayato was unable to predict.

"Ayato, are you okay?" Haruka called out to him as she circled around her father.

The fact that their opponent was giving them this opportunity to regroup was no doubt a sign of his absolute confidence in his own abilities.

"Haruka, take this!" Ayato said, handing her his spare Lux.

Haruka's own Lux had been damaged in their last exchange. Sparks were flying from its manadite core, its blade wavering as if it might go out at any moment. By the looks of things, normal Luxes didn't stand much of a chance against the Raksha-Nada.

"Thanks," she said in a low voice as she took Ayato's spare in her hands. "This isn't good. He's much stronger now than he was the last time I fought him."

"...Where do you think it comes from, his strength?" Ayato whispered back to her.

There was no mistaking that Lamina Mortis's combat techniques were far superior to his and Haruka's. Ayato had no idea how old their opponent was, but it was inevitable that he would have accumulated a lot of experience over those years.

That didn't mean, however, that he and Haruka were out of options.

"Hmm, probably his prana," Haruka responded under her breath.

"His prana?"

Ayato looked over their overly calm opponent with fresh eyes. Mortis undoubtedly excelled at controlling his prana, but in terms of quantity, it was still Ayato who had the advantage.

"Not the amount. It's different in quality," Haruka continued. "This is only a guess, but I think his savagery is feeding into it. Compared with ours, his is much more compact, much denser."

"What?"

Ayato had never heard anything like this before.

In the first place, their opponent's savage nature was ultimately nothing more than a mental attitude. Of course, that in itself could have an effect on one's strength, but it shouldn't have been able to change the quality of his prana.

Stregas and Dantes might be able to control their abilities through willpower alone, but this...

At that moment, he suddenly remembered something that Eishirou had told him a while back.

"They say Stregas and Dantes make up just a few percent of

Genestella, right? In reality, though, lots of people have a natural ability to link with mana but can't express it as special powers—either because they're too weak or because they can't visualize what they want to do. According to some, more Genestella have that basic ability than not."

Prana was, after all, the source of a Genestella's power. It could be used to increase the strength of one's attacks, to raise one's defense, and, depending on how it was used, even to boost one's speed.

On top of that, Mortis's brand of viciousness was composed of an intrinsic desire to crush his foes, born of the most basic negative emotions such as anger and hatred.

Assuming that this incredibly powerful savagery of his could indeed affect his prana, it wasn't hard to imagine just how profound a change it would cause.

Ayato could only wonder just what could lie at the heart of such intense emotions.

"It's time. Enough with the games, Lamina Mortis." Varda, until now watching on in silence, stepped forward, her voice reproachful.

"...I see." Lamina Mortis gave a brief nod. "Indeed, it is. We had better move things along," he said with a grin as he directed the Raksha-Nada toward Ayato.

"Well then, wielder of the Ser Veresta. The Four Colored Runeswords each have unique abilities, but they are all similarly ineffective against their brethren. The Ser Veresta has the power to burn through all of creation; the Lei-Glems the power to make contact only with its intended target; the Wole-Zain the ability to cut through space at any specified coordinates... And I'm sure you know just what the Raksha-Nada is capable of?"

Before Ayato's eyes, the blade began to split into countless tiny shards, the pieces separating again into even smaller fragments, until Lamina Mortis was left holding nothing but an oversized hilt.

Now, in place of its blade, what emerged in front of him resembled only a crimson mist.

"...Haruka, get behind me."

"Right." She wasted no time in doing as he had told her.

They both, of course, knew about the Raksha-Nada.

It was getting ready for a *full-surface slash.*

"Arghhhhhhhhhh!"

Ayato poured his prana into the Ser Veresta as Lamina Mortis swung the hilt of the Orga Lux forward with a tremendous roar.

Ayato's blade swelled to enormous proportions as he stabbed it into the ground. He crouched behind it like a shield.

Not a moment later, he was swallowed in a cloud of red light as the innumerable fragments of the Raksha-Nada swept past him.

"Oh? Well done. Perhaps you *do* know how to use the Ser Veresta." Mortis's voice was tinged with admiration.

Ayato turned around. Haruka had crouched down, covering her face with her hands, but fortunately, she appeared to be unharmed.

Farther behind them, though, the abandoned building that had been standing there until just a moment ago was now torn to shreds, having collapsed into a pile of rubble and dust.

"How can it be this powerful…?"

Ayato had, of course, read about the Raksha-Nada, but this was his first time seeing its abilities in action. The fact that it had seldom been put to actual use was, of course, partly due to the debilitating cost that the Orga Lux demanded, but it was also no doubt that the weapon's sheer cruelty and destructive potential had played a part. Ayato may have been able to shield himself from the attack thanks to the Ser Veresta, but any other opponent would have been torn to shreds. It wasn't difficult to imagine that any typical usage of the weapon would be a direct violation of the Stella Carta.

"Haruka, stay close to me," Ayato said as he retrieved the Ser Veresta—to no response.

"Haruka…?"

At that instant, a terrible, nauseating premonition welled up inside him. He spun back around, when—

"U-ugh…!" Haruka's face was a picture of agony as she fell to the ground, clutching at her chest.

"Haruka!" Ayato took her in his arms at once, calling out to her, but she appeared to be unable to respond. "Haruka, hang in there!"

He looked her over for injuries, but nothing stood out. There wasn't even any sign of blood.

"I told you, didn't I? I came here to threaten you. Think of this as a demonstration," Lamina Mortis said coldly.

The crimson mist was once again gathering around the Orga Lux's hilt.

"Normally, when it's broken down into small pieces like this, the shards of the Raksha-Nada can only be controlled as a whole...but I do have some room to freely move them. Like this."

One of the red shards began to move in the opposite direction from the others, emerging out from the cloud and expanding to the size of a fingernail.

"What have you done to her?!"

"Ha-ha, I haven't done anything to her, at least not today. No, this is from our encounter at the Eclipse."

"!"

The fragment returned to the cloud, which soon condensed back into a blade—or so Ayato thought, but another piece, around the size of a pinky finger, remained hovering above the palm of Lamina Mortis's outstretched hand.

"That day...after I cut her down...I had a fragment implanted inside her body, you see. Ah, you needn't worry about her life. That isn't in danger—so long as I don't move it." He paused there, pinching the remaining fragment with his fingers.

"Aaaaaaaaaaaagh!" Haruka screamed, her voice pure agony.

"Haruka! Haruka!" Ayato cried out, deactivating his sword. "Stop it, Mortis! You win!"

"A wise decision. Let me add one more thing. I think you'll find that removing that fragment will be remarkably difficult. It will only be there, physically inside her, while the Raksha-Nada is activated." Mortis began to walk toward them, his cold eyes peering down through his mask at the both of them. "I want to keep from killing you, Haruka. I really do. But I won't take any second chances, I'm afraid. Thanks to you, our best plan, our fastest, most elegant one, has come to nothing. Our present efforts may pale in comparison to what we had hoped to achieve, but I won't let you interfere with them again. If you try to oppose us this time, I'll show you no mercy." He spoke plainly, his tone matter-of-fact, but it was clear that he meant every word.

If they tried anything, Ayato understood, he no doubt meant to kill her.

"...I'll enter the Lindvolus. That's what you want, isn't it?"

"No, I'm afraid that alone won't be enough. It would be such a killjoy if you were to lose during in the first round, for instance. I'm going to have to insist that you take the championship."

"What...?!"

In other words, he would have to defeat Erenshkigal.

Moreover, that could mean having to fight Julis, too.

"It shouldn't be impossible for you, given your abilities. Together, I want the two of you to show the world the glory that is your birthright. How about it? Do you have a problem with any of that?"

"...Fine." Ayato bit his lips, all but dragging the answer out of his throat.

He had no choice but to submit.

"Haruka, I'm going to need you to remove my seal. It isn't that we need my strength to carry out the plan or anything...but it is a nuisance. If you've made it somewhat irregular, like last time, we're going to have a problem."

Haruka scowled up at him, but her eyes were filled with resignation. After a short moment, she shut her eyes, letting out a hopeless sigh. "*With this I do dispel thy fetters and release thy power,*" she murmured under her breath.

As the words faded into silence, Ayato could practically see the weight of the invisible chains that had been holding Lamina Mortis back completely vanishing.

"Thank you. That's one problem taken care of," he said as he turned his back on them, his voice seemingly reinvigorated. "I can't say I don't want you to come back...but I'm afraid that would ruffle the feathers of my associates. You wanted to enter Stjarnagarm, if I'm not mistaken. Well, I won't stand in your way."

"...You won't stop her?" Ayato called back in bewilderment.

"Whether she joins them or not, nothing will change," Lamina Mortis answered without even looking back. "The same goes for you, Ayato. Did you think I didn't know about your little conspiracy with the Enfields and Miss Lyyneheym? As ineffective as they are, I suspect they will keep doing what they're doing, with or without your help. And putting aside Miss Enfield and Miss Lyyneheym, neither the elder Enfield nor the commander of Stjarnagarm would be foolish enough to oppose us directly. But if you did try, I suppose I could always use the Raksha-Nada."

Lamina Mortis, it seemed, already knew everything.

As he turned to leave, Ayato called out in desperation: "What the hell are you trying to achieve? Even before all this, you went and kidnapped Haruka, you tried to cause a second Invertia, and then you attacked me before the last match of the Gryps to do what? Give me a bit more experience? It doesn't make any sense!"

"What am I trying to achieve? Hmm, if I had to say...I'm just trying to speed things along a little."

That answer was so far from what Ayato had been expecting that he had no idea what to make of it.

"'Speed things along'...?"

"Exactly. That's all I'm after," Lamina Mortis declared, before disappearing with Varda into the darkness of the ruins.

*

At almost the exact same time, in a different section of the redevelopment area—

"To think that *you* would have called *me* here, Orphelia." Julis fought to keep her emotions in check as she called out to her friend.

"No matter how many times I tried to reach you, you kept on turning me down. And now this turn of events."

Orphelia stood alone in the center of a ruined building, the roof of which had completely fallen in. The moonlight combing through her glistening white hair; her crimson eyes staring directly at Julis; and her voice, as she responded to her, seemed to be filled with unfathomable sorrow: "...This is our fate, Julis."

"Hmph, fate again? Unfortunately for you, I don't believe in that overly romantic notion."

The school fair had been running today, but Julis had spent practically the whole day in her training room, working to improve her control over her prana in whatever small way she could.

It wasn't as if she hadn't thought about spending the day with Ayato...but Haruka had only just returned to Asterisk, and she didn't want to make a nuisance of herself.

But then Orphelia had reached out to her.

"You know, you could have picked somewhere a little nicer. Or did you want to come here on purpose?"

This whole place was filled with painful memories. They were standing in the very location where Julis had first reunited with Orphelia, where they had fought against each other for the first time, and where Julis had been soundly defeated.

"I chose a place we both know. That was all."

"...Right. Well, what did you want to tell me?"

Orphelia would hardly have called her here just to remind her of that nightmarish experience. If she was being honest with herself, there was nothing Julis wanted more right now than to drag Orphelia from the mire of deception and conflict that she had found herself in and take her back to Lieseltania—but she knew that would be impossible.

She still wasn't strong enough to do that.

As she was now, she still couldn't get through to her.

"Can I ask you something first?" Orphelia asked. "Why are you so obsessed with me?"

"Isn't it obvious? Because you're my dear, precious friend," Julis answered without the slightest hesitation.

"…I see. We *were* friends. But it's different now."

"!"

Julis gritted her teeth but forced herself to take a deep breath. "…If you had come to this city of your own free will, if you had chosen to serve the Tyrant, that would be one thing. I might not have wanted to accept it, but the pain would have been that of friends going separate ways. But that isn't what happened. You've given up on your own free will, on your own desires. You're letting yourself be manipulated by this illusion you call *fate*. So I'm going to save you, no matter what it takes. I'll meet your challenge."

That day, during their first meeting at Asterisk, Orphelia had said to her that if her fate could surpass her own, then she would do as Julis wished. All she had to do was break the school crest hanging from her chest.

"Yes, I did say that. But the situation has changed. That's what I wanted to tell you."

"What's that supposed to mean?"

Orphelia's unblinking eyes were filled with resignation and sorrow. "My end is drawing near. If you want to overturn my fate…please kill me. Let me die by your hand."

"What?! How could I…?!"

At that moment, the air around Orphelia, almost trembling with an incredible amount of mana, suddenly erupted, with countless miasmic arms rising up from the ground.

"!" Julis didn't waste a moment before activating her Rect Lux. "What are you doing? Don't tell me you want this again?"

"…Let's put your fate to the test, Julis."

Those brackish, corpse-like arms tore through the ground like a gale as they raced toward Julis. But before they could reach her—

"Burst into bloom—*Moss Phlox!*"

Julis's ability burned through them all in the blink of an eye, leaving only countless pink-colored embers dancing through the air like petals.

This was a new technique, one that required the use of her Rect Lux. In short, she used its remote terminals, deployed around her in perfect formation, to help channel her prana, greatly amplifying the efficiency and range of her attacks.

"...Well, Orphelia? I've grown since we last fought. And I've got new techniques, ones that I didn't use at the Gryps."

"Hmm..." Orphelia's sorrowful expression remained unchanged as she let out a deep sigh. "Your fate certainly glows brighter now than it did before. So let me ask you again. Julis...please kill me."

"Don't even joke about that!"

This time, she couldn't hold herself back. As she cried out in anger, she stepped forward, reaching to grab Orphelia by the collar, when—

"I'm not joking." Orphelia's whole body seemed to waver like a mirage, when all of a sudden, she was standing not in front of Julis, but at her side.

How did she...?!

Before Julis could even move, she leaned forward to whisper in her ear:

"____________________"

"What?!"

Julis could do nothing but stand dumbfounded, doubting her own hearing. Orphelia's words had been that shocking.

"W-wait! I don't believe you! That doesn't make any sense! What would be the point of doing something like that...?!" she whispered, her voice pained.

Orphelia was turning to leave, when she paused to look back. "I don't know. But the reason is irrelevant. All that matters is that it's my fate," she replied, her voice bearing all the anguish of someone condemned to hell and, at the same time, a detached matter-of-factness, as if she weren't even talking about herself.

She was being completely serious.

As soon as Julis realized that, an anger so powerful that it all but blotted out her sense of consternation erupted from deep inside her.

"Orphelia!"

Julis reached out toward her, but before her fingertips could graze against her pure white hair, Julis was slammed completely into the ground.

"Guh...?!"

It wasn't an attack from Orphelia's miasma. Julis had been on her guard against her abilities.

No, she remembered this feeling, this sense of being crushed by a gigantic, unseen weight. She had experienced it once before.

She managed, with difficulty, to look upward, only to see *it* gripped tightly in Orphelia's hand.

"Wh-why...do you...have...that...?!" She had to practically wring every word from her throat.

Orphelia, on the other hand, wore a grave expression as she stroked its blade. "Because I was ordered to. This one also suffers."

It was an enormous scythe.

There was no way that Julis could have forgotten the eerie purple hue of its urm-manadite core.

The Gravisheath.

The last time she had encountered this notorious Orga Lux with the ability to manipulate gravity, it had been in the hands of Irene Urzaiz from Le Wolfe, when she had fought against her during the Phoenix. It was supposed to have been destroyed by Ayato at the end of the match—but looking closer, she could tell it had changed. It must have been reassembled.

The biggest difference was, unmistakably, its aura.

During the Phoenix, the Orga Lux had seemed to be looking down on Julis and Ayato—and even Irene, its own user—with contempt. It had clearly harbored a sense of malice toward people.

Now, however, all that seemed to have been replaced with shrieks of agony. That violet urm-manadite core was, in its own way, crying out for help.

"She doesn't like my blood, it seems."

The cost of using the Gravisheath was precisely that—blood.

Orphelia's, however, was highly toxic—so much so that one drop would be enough to kill everything growing in the ground below.

"...But thanks to that, she's very docile. Completely different from what Irene Urzaiz told me about her."

In other words, Orphelia had been able to make the Gravisheath submit to her will.

Generally speaking, Stregas and Dantes didn't have strong affinities with Orga Luxes, but it was true that a very small number of such individuals had been able to successfully enter the Festa. Haruka, wielding the Ser Veresta, was one such example.

And yet—

So now I've got another hurdle to overcome...?!

Orphelia was the two-time champion of the Lindvolus and, perhaps, the strongest Strega in history. Even if she didn't wield an Orga Lux, there was no one truly capable of challenging her throne.

"...You mustn't tell anyone about this, Julis. If word were to get out, they'll move their plans forward ahead of the tournament," Orphelia said in warning as she began to depart.

"W-wait...! Orphelia...!" Julis reached out desperately toward her, but it wasn't enough.

It had never been enough.

Even after the weight of the Gravisheath had completely dissipated, Julis couldn't muster the will to pull herself up from the ground.

Flames of bitter frustration, of anger, of despair raged inside her as she turned the same thoughts over and over again.

Why had Orphelia told her all that if she didn't want anyone else to know?

Why had she gone out of her way to call her here in the first place?

"...Orphelia!" she called out again, clenching her outstretched fist.

Perhaps, Julis wondered, she was deceiving herself.

But she was sure of it: Orphelia had wanted this meeting.

And if that was the case, then this was no time to lay sprawled here in despair.

She rose to her feet, resolve flowing through her anew. After passing one last glance down the pathway through which Orphelia had disappeared, the princess spun around, determined to put these ruins behind her.

CHAPTER 7
PREPARING FOR BATTLE

"...What's this about?" Saya demanded with suspicion as she entered the room at the Hotel Elnath.

"Th-this is..." Kirin, coming in behind her, raised her hand to her mouth in surprise.

"Welcome, you two. Thank you for coming," Claudia said with her usual open smile.

Ayato grinned back at them nervously from his seat on the sofa at the back of the room, while beside him, Haruka's expression was one of warmth.

The source of their confusion was on the other side of the room. On the sofa at the opposite side of the table sat Sylvia Lyyneheym, alias Sigrdrífa, waving at them; while leaning against the wall with her arms crossed was the commander of Stjarnagarm, Helga Lindwall.

"We're all here now." Then, from the adjoining room, came a blond woman in a black suit.

"Saya Sasamiya, and Kirin Toudou. My name is Isabella Enfield. Pleased to meet you."

"Enfield?" Kirin repeated. "You mean...?"

"Yes, I'm Claudia's mother. It's a pleasure," Isabella replied as she held out her hand to them, her countenance practically a mirror-image of her daughter's.

"Y-yes...," Kirin stammered as she shook her hand.

Saya, however, pursed her lips. "I don't know what's going on, but I came here because Ayato said it was important. I want an explanation."

Nor did she understand why Julis was absent from the group.

If it was as important as Ayato had made out, then she should have been the first to come to his help. Judging by the situation, Saya got the impression that she wouldn't be joining them later, either.

"Please, take a seat," Claudia urged them, motioning toward an empty sofa. "Ayato wasn't lying when he called you. Although it did take us some time to convince him that we should bring you all in."

Ayato nodded. "I'm still against it. I don't want to drag either of you into this, Saya, Kirin. There's no going back once we get started, so please, think about it carefully before—"

"It's fine. Go on," Saya said without the slightest hesitation.

"...Please." Kirin nodded in agreement.

That should have been obvious. If Ayato was in trouble, nothing could stand in the way of their helping him.

"This really is dangerous," he continued, his expression grave. "I mean—"

"I told you, didn't I?" Claudia said, patting him on the shoulder. "Neither Saya nor Kirin is the kind of person to turn their back on you."

"How nice," Sylvia said, chuckling. "They must really love you, Ayato."

"...Sigrdrífa. How lucky. I've been wanting to meet you for some time."

"Sylvie is fine. But what for?"

At this, Saya leaned forward, looking her over distrustfully. "If you're just messing around with Ayato, I want you to leave him alone."

"Oh my, what an awful thing to say. I'm completely serious about him. And do I really need your permission to get involved with him?"

"Of course."

"And why would that be?"

"Because I've known him forever," Saya stated flatly, sticking out her chest.

"...That isn't a particularly good reason," Sylvia replied, returning a sharp look. "But what makes you think I'm the problem? If I'm not mistaken, Miss Toudou and Ayato stayed at each other's houses over the New Year. Maybe you should be more worried about her."

"Whaaat?!"

"I haven't forgotten about that, either..."

"N-no, like I said, that was..." Kirin, suddenly finding herself at the center of the conversation, tried to blunder out an explanation.

"Ah, speaking of which, Dad spoke pretty highly of you, Kirin," Haruka interrupted. "He thought you were very considerate."

"Eh? Th-that's... I'm honored!" Her face turned bright red under the praise as she stared at her feet. It was clear from the pleased ring to her voice that she wasn't as flustered as she would have them all believe.

"*Ngh*... I guess this is what they mean by that saying. 'He that would the daughter win, must with the mother first begin,' huh...?"

"Ah-ha-ha! In that case, I'll just have to get his sister on my side..." Sylvia leaned forward with excitement, grabbing Haruka by the hand. "What do you say? Why don't we go out for tea sometime? I'd love to hear what Ayato was like as a kid."

"Oh my, I'm honored to be invited by the world's most popular songstress. I have to admit, I'm interested in you too, Sylvia," Haruka replied with a laugh as she gripped her hand back.

"Sylvia, if you want to hear about Ayato's childhood, I'm sure that Saya will be able to satisfy you," Claudia interrupted, joining the fray.

"Oh? Bring it on." Saya beckoned toward her. "I could go on for three days and nights."

"What would be the point in that?" Sylvia shook her head, frowning.

"Um... Sorry about this, but do you mind if we move on to why you called us all here?" With the situation getting out of hand,

Helga, with a look of bafflement, somehow managed to bring the room back under control.

"That's all we know about the Golden Bough Alliance and their current activities," Isabella finished, having summarized everything that had happened thus far.

"That's..." Kirin had raised her hands to her face, as if she could hardly believe what she had just heard. "How could they use Haruka's life as a bargaining chip...?"

"Hmm... This Lamina Mortis is one thing, but the Varda-Vaos's abilities sound extraordinary...," Saya murmured.

Indeed, if it was the Orga Lux's energy output that gave it the power to interfere with people's thoughts, then not even a Genestella normally resistant to mind control would be able to withstand it.

On top of that, the body that it had currently usurped was that of Sylvia Lyyneheym's former teacher.

By the sound of it, all of their problems were tangled up with one another.

Isabella gave Saya and Kirin a moment to digest everything before asking: "Do you understand our position now, and why we asked you all to come here in secret?"

"...I understand," Saya answered. "This Golden Bough Alliance is a serious danger. And Ayato will have to enter the Lindvolus."

If Haruka's life depended on it, then he had no choice.

"I have some questions, though."

"If I can answer them, I will," Isabella replied with a composed smile.

"Firstly, why exactly were we all called to this meeting? The Varda-Vaos is supposed to be top secret, so Galaxy shouldn't want information on it spreading unnecessarily. On top of that..." She paused there, glancing toward Helga.

It could turn bad for Galaxy if the head of Stjarnagarm shared that information with her colleagues.

"Ah, you don't need to worry about the commander here. We've already made all the necessary political arrangements."

"...I can't say I'm happy about them, though," Helga murmured.

"Of course, your concerns are reasonable, Miss Sasamiya. At Galaxy, we certainly want to make sure that knowledge about the Varda-Vaos stays in the hands of as few individuals as possible. However, I'm afraid that circumstances have already moved on to the next stage."

"Because I woke up, you mean?" Haruka asked with a reluctant smile.

"Exactly. The information that Haruka provided came as a great surprise to us. As such, we revised and presented our threat evaluation of the Golden Bough Alliance to the executive committee, and they have decided to review our approach with the Varda-Vaos. As it happened, the commander already had a thorough grasp of the situation, so now that we've got several conditions out of the way, we have decided to establish a united front."

"And those conditions are?" Saya asked bluntly.

"That I, as well as Haruka—although she hasn't formally joined us yet—won't share this information with any other members of the guard," Helga answered with a shrug. "That we'll keep all this secret, that we'll hand over the Varda-Vaos once it's secured, and so on."

"...And you're okay with that?"

To be honest, Saya wouldn't have expected her to agree to those kinds of terms. As commander of the city guard, Helga Lindwall was renowned for her sense of honesty and honor. She wasn't normally the kind of person to make such a deal.

Perhaps having guessed what Saya was thinking, Helga let out a deep sigh. "Don't look at me like that. The highest priority of all of us at Stjarnagarm is the protection of this city. If this information was made public, and the power balance among the integrated enterprise foundations fell into disarray, all of Asterisk would soon follow suit. It's my duty to prevent that from happening."

"A wise decision," Isabella added.

Helga, however, cast her a sharp gaze. "Of course, that doesn't mean I'm going to overlook any illegal activities. I'm simply prioritizing stopping Lamina Mortis and the Varda-Vaos. Once that's taken care of, we're going to have to settle our accounts with Galaxy, too. That's why I agreed to this."

"Well, that is a separate matter," Isabella replied, returning Helga's look. The intensity of their gazes as they stared each other down was almost enough to set off sparks.

"U-um...," Kirin began timidly, raising her hand. "But why were *we* called here?"

"Because you've already heard Haruka's version of what happened, and we decided it would be easier to bring you in fully rather than risk leaving you unsupervised with only a partial understanding of the situation. The executive committee was divided on this matter, so I've taken personal responsibility. I'm looking forward to your cooperation," Isabella said, bowing her head.

"Wh-what...? Don't say that!" Kirin shrank back for a moment but gradually relaxed as she seemed to understand what exactly she meant.

Galaxy no doubt needed to increase the number of pieces on its side of the board, Saya surmised, but was unable to bring its own units in.

"...What exactly do you want us to do?" she asked.

"For now, just collect information. Anything you can relating to Lamina Mortis or the Varda-Vaos. For example... The Raksha-Nada is one clue. The Orga Lux is the property of Le Wolfe and is supposed to have been sealed away. And yet, it's clearly in the possession of Mortis. We need to know how."

"Can't you check that with Le Wolfe directly?" Kirin asked, putting into words the very doubt that Saya herself had been harboring.

This time, it was Claudia's turn to respond. "Unfortunately, they are under no obligation to respond to queries from students belonging to other schools, nor from the city guard, for that matter. They will no doubt ignore any queries that we might make. Although it would, of course, be different if Solnage were to get involved..."

"But if its whereabouts have been deliberately covered up, doesn't that mean Le Wolfe must be involved as well?" Sylvia pointed out.

"Le Wolfe was closely involved in the Eclipse, so we can't discount that possibility," Helga answered. "And yet…it's difficult to believe that the school itself is working with the Golden Bough Alliance. It's possible that they have a collaborator in a position overseeing their inventory of Orga Luxes. And, of course…the Varda-Vaos itself has the power to turn just about anyone into a coconspirator."

"…There's quite a lot that we would like you to do, from following up on leads like this, to inspecting the place where Ayato and Haruka encountered Lamina Mortis and the Varda-Vaos. Especially now that we have much more data on the man's past activities thanks to Haruka here," Isabella said with a clap as she summed up their various options.

"We would like to locate them before the Lindvolus, if possible," Claudia added. "We don't know precisely what their goal is, but if they're willing to go this far to force Ayato to participate in the tournament, then their plans must be timed to coincide."

"Ah…!" Saya startled, suddenly realizing something. "Then, if we can't deal with them before that, maybe it would be best if I pulled out?"

If they couldn't stop Mortis before the Lindvolus, then Ayato would have no choice but to win the tournament. If she and Ayato were forced to face off against each other, that would only get in the way of things.

It pained her to have to break her promise with Camilla, but as vexing as that was, Haruka's life was more important.

"Ah, right. I guess I should do that, too." Sylvia clapped her hand against her forehead, as if having realized the same thing. "It'd be a shame to miss my chance at getting revenge on Orphelia, but if this is how things are, well, there's no helping it."

"…I'm really sorry," Ayato said, bowing his head.

"Really, really sorry," Haruka added, following suit.

It wasn't the fault of either of them—Saya didn't need to be told that. If she was going to blame anyone, it would be the Golden Bough Alliance.

"No, I think it would be best if you both entered the tournament as planned," Claudia interrupted with a cool smile. "Neither of you are aiming for the top, if I'm not mistaken. You both want to defeat specific opponents, no? There's every possibility that you would be able to do that before possibly facing Ayato. Not only that, but it would, of course, be a great help to him if you could defeat as many potential obstacles as possible."

Of course... Saya was shocked that she hadn't thought of that herself.

"And if you do end up facing him, you can always withdraw from the match. That would be much better than not entering the tournament at all."

"B-besides, we might find a way to remove that piece of the Raksha-Nada from Haruka's body before the Lindvolus!" Kirin added, clenching her fists in front of her chest.

"I'm afraid I don't know what our chances of success are as far as that's concerned, but I'm having Director Korbel look into it. Although I should say he didn't seem particularly optimistic," Isabella told them.

As harsh as her words were, it was no doubt better than getting their hopes up unnecessarily.

"...One last question," Saya began, turning away from Isabella and Claudia and toward Ayato. "Why isn't Julis here?"

Kirin was startled at this one, looking over the room once more as if she hadn't realized Julis's absence until now.

Indeed, Julis's absence troubled Saya the most.

Given her personality, she, like the others, could have been expected to do whatever was in her power to help Ayato.

Nevertheless, she was the only one of them not present.

"...I told Julis the situation a little earlier. I left out the stuff about the Varda-Vaos, but I did tell her I would be entering the Lindvolus for Haruka's sake." Ayato fell silent there, a pained expression settling over his face.

Ayato had been saying for seemingly forever now that he wanted to be Julis's strength, to help her however he could. That was why he had originally decided not to enter the tournament in the first place.

For him to break that promise now was no doubt a cause of considerable shame for him.

"And what did Julis say…?"

"…I think it came as a shock to her. She said she wanted to be left alone for a while," Ayato replied, biting his lip.

"That…doesn't sound like her," Claudia commented.

"I thought she would have been concerned for you and Haruka…," Kirin added.

Saya was of the same mind. She knew how obsessed Julis was about facing her childhood friend Orphelia Landlufen. Doing so had been at the forefront of her thoughts for as long as she had known her. Nonetheless, despite all that, Saya would have expected her to come to the same conclusion as she and Sylvia.

And yet—

"Anyway, I want to respect her feelings," Ayato said, closing his eyes as he gripped his fists tightly.

For Saya, just seeing Ayato like this was painful. For some reason, as she stared across the room at him, she felt her own chest tightening, overcome by a wave of emotions that threatened to make her break down into tears.

*

Julis was sitting alone in her training room, curled up into a ball by the far wall.

The only spot of light in the almost pitch-black room was a small flame, conjured up by her abilities. The dim light left her expression looking dark and sullen.

"…Why?" She herself hardly heard the faint whisper that emanated from her lips.

Naturally, there was no one in that dark silence who could have responded to her.

"Is this the fate that you keep mentioning, Orphelia…?"

But, of course, there was no answer.

"In that case…" She paused there, clenching her teeth.

Tears were welling in her eyes.

"What exactly am I supposed to do...?!"

Still casting her head downward, she slammed her fist against the wall, a dull thud echoing across the room.

"..."

She had no idea how long she had been sitting there like this.

She rubbed at her eyes with the back of her hands before slowly rising to her feet.

At the same time, countless small flames burst into light around her.

There were well over a thousand of them in total.

"...How am I supposed to make up my mind?!"

How could she be expected to choose?

All she could do was follow through with what she had already started, no matter how much it ate at her.

That was the only real option left to her now.

*

They were on a small outdoor stage in the corner of a park located in the commercial area. There were, of course, no defensive barriers or any such advanced facilities at a stage like this—rather, it was enclosed only a by low-lying physical wall.

"...Your uniform suits you."

"Do you think so? Ha-ha, thanks. Well, I'm not officially enlisted until tomorrow, so it's still just for show... I wanted to show it to you, though."

In the center of the stage, Ayato and Haruka were chatting idly as they did their prematch stretches.

He, of course, was dressed in his Seidoukan uniform. Haruka, on the other hand, having easily passed the recruitment exam, was clothed in the formal uniform of an officer of Stjarnagarm.

It was eight o'clock in the evening, and seeing as they were some distance from the business areas, there was no one else in sight.

"Well, should we get started? Can you lend me the Ser Veresta for a second?"

"Right," Ayato murmured, removing the Orga Lux from its holder at his waist, before activating it and handing it over to her.

"Sorry, Ser Veresta," Haruka whispered to it. "This will probably be a little uncomfortable, but it will only take a little while."

Chains of mana flowed from her hand and then across the blade, wrapping themselves around it as the seal took hold.

"...Hmm, this should do it. I don't think it will last for very long, but this should seal away the sharpness of the Ser Veresta at least for a little while. We wouldn't be able to train properly otherwise."

Ayato could only look on with admiration. "I had no idea your ability could do this... You really are amazing, Haruka."

In principle, Orga Luxes greatly exceeded the abilities of Dantes and Stregas in power. They were simply too different in the ways that they manifested themselves. Even if it was only temporary, the fact that Haruka could even do this at all was nothing short of incredible.

"It only worked because Ser Veresta is willing to cooperate. If it wasn't, there's no way the seal would hold," Haruka said, waving her hands as if to brush away the praise.

In other words, the Ser Veresta trusted her. That, too, was almost unbelievable. He knew firsthand how difficult the Orga Lux could be to please.

"Are you ready, Ayato? Like I told you earlier, you've never been very good at properly controlling your prana. But we won't have time before the Lindvolus if we start right from the very beginning."

"...That's why we're using the Ser Veresta, then?"

In other words, he didn't need versatility.

It would be enough if he could properly handle the Orga Lux.

"First, you're going to need to have mastered Ser Veresta. You've always been the kind of person who learns through practice, so we're just going to have to jump right into it. Are you okay with that?"

"Yeah, I'm ready."

The two of them took their positions before bowing toward one another and adopting fighting stances. Ayato held the Ser Veresta in front of him; Haruka, her blade-type Lux over her shoulder.

"I'm not going to hold back. There would be no point to this if I did."

"I wouldn't want you to," Ayato answered.

No sooner did he finish speaking than Haruka rushed toward him.

"Umph!"

Ayato stepped back, hoping to avoid her diagonal overhead slash, but as she closed in, the tip of her blade flashed in front of him before darting down straight into his chest.

The Amagiri Shinmei Style, Middle Technique—Twin Serpents, Recapitulation...?!

He shifted his body with the Ser Veresta in an attempt to evade her attack, but Haruka wasn't about to let him get away. She moved to the side, closing in around him, to prevent him from putting any distance between the two of them.

At their current positions, it was clear that Haruka had the advantage. The Ser Veresta was too large for him to match the speed of her blade. It seemed she was trying to force him to up his game by staying as close as possible.

As he should have expected, she was showing him no mercy.

He dodged her next strike, a low slash, while at the same time realizing that she was holding her weapon single-handed. As a result of that, her movements were slightly slower than usual. He moved reflexively to counter, when she reached with her left hand behind her back and—

She activated a second blade.

"!"

Ayato raised the Ser Veresta desperately to shield himself.

"Haaah!"

She swung down first with her right hand and then cut back across from the left with it. She spun around and then lunged forward, cutting down diagonally with the left blade and slashing across with the right. Haruka spun around once more, stabbing toward him with her left, until finally stepping yet closer and, with her right-hand blade, launching into the Amagiri Shinmei Twin Sword Style, Middle Technique—*Hell Spider.*

Ayato, withstanding the sequence of seven consecutive attacks, still couldn't pull away from Haruka, who came now rushing toward him with her twin swords reversed, poised to slam the pommels of both blades into either side of his body.

"Ngh...!"

It was a grappling technique from the Amagiri Shinmei style—Grindstone Pommel, Strata.

There was no way that he could have avoided this move. His only option was to focus his prana and hope that he could withstand it.

But Haruka didn't stop there, spinning her blades around back to their normal position and swinging them toward his shoulders like scythes.

This was Twin Serpents, a dual-sword technique from the Amagiri Shinmei style—but this time, Ayato managed to parry the move at the last possible moment before taking advantage of the brief opening to pull himself away and regain his defensive stance.

"Haaah...! Haaah...!" His breath was ragged.

"Just like I thought. The Ser Veresta hasn't fully accepted you."

With that, Haruka returned the Lux in her left hand to its holder at her waist and adopted a two-handed posture with her remaining blade.

"That's a bit harsh, Haruka...!"

According to what she told him when she had woken up, he was supposed to have reached her own level of ability back when he had unlocked his third seal.

While it was true that her assault was giving him few opportunities to counter, and that the sheer size of the Ser Veresta was one contributing factor to that, he couldn't deny that she was simply more proficient at the Amagiri Shinmei style. If they were to fight with the same weapons, using the same techniques, she would undoubtedly get the better of him. Ayato, who had only been taught the basics by his father, Masatsugu, couldn't hope to match her in that regard.

To begin with, Haruka had already mastered almost all of the Amagiri Shinmei style's various techniques. As a rule, students of the style weren't permitted to study other weapons, such as the spear or the short sword, until they had mastered the sword techniques up to at least the middle level. The grappling techniques in particular were a necessary building block before one could master the hidden techniques. While Ayato had learned both the sword and the grappling techniques to a considerable level, he was still studying the others (although it was true that Masatsugu had taught him the basics of wielding two blades simultaneously).

The two of them were practically equal in overall strength, but as far as physical stamina was concerned, Ayato was no doubt ahead. In an actual battle, Ayato would probably have been able to emerge victorious.

However—if he couldn't adjust the Ser Veresta to an optimal size, he wouldn't be able to control the most essential component of all his techniques, which would leave him with little chance of turning his current situation around.

"Let me give you some advice," his sister said. "What's the Ser Veresta to you? Think about that."

"What is it to me…?"

Ayato had no idea what she meant.

"If you don't know that—no, if you can't feel that—it won't stay with you for very long."

Haruka wasn't the kind of person to prolong a match just to tease her opponents. She was no doubt planning to deal the final blow.

No sooner had that thought run through his head than she began to shuffle toward him, narrowing the distance between them, when, as expected, she launched into another full-frontal assault.

She swooped toward him from above, from below—from every possible direction with an almost godlike speed.

That's the Amagiri Shinmei Style, Middle Technique—Spiraling Whirlpool…! And the First Technique—Scarlet Saber! And another Middle Technique—Saddle of Knowledge!

He only barely managed to catch the moves with the Ser Veresta thanks to the sheer size of the weapon. It was clear, however, that at this rate, Haruka would keep chipping down at his defenses until he could no longer resist.

Of course, Ayato wasn't devoting everything he had to defense. While holding Haruka off, he poured his prana into the Orga Lux's urm-manadite core, trying every possible technique he could think of to try to make it take on a more optimal size.

No matter what he did, however, he couldn't bring it under control.

While controlling one's prana was often compared to threading a needle, given the sheer quantity of Ayato's prana, it was much more like trying for force a rope through the eye of one—in other words, all but impossible.

This is bad...! Any more of this, and...

Haruka's attacks continued to increase in speed and intensity. By the way she was managing to stay one step ahead of him, she looked to be reading his every movement.

Ayato might have grown considerably from how she remembered him, but given that she was the one who had taught him most of what he knew of the Amagiri Shinmei style, it was perhaps inevitable that she would be able to see through his actions.

For his part, Ayato knew Haruka's fighting style all too well, but as far as raw speed was concerned, he was simply no match for her.

"Ngh...!"

The tip of her blade tore through his uniform, leaving blood oozing from a light wound.

She certainly wasn't going easy on him, but this was still just a training bout. She had probably pulled back at the last minute to keep from seriously injuring him, although given Ayato's prana, it was unlikely that a slash from a regular Lux would cause too much damage.

In any event, if he couldn't win here, he wouldn't stand a chance against Orphelia.

Nor would he have any hope of defeating Lamina Mortis.

I'm not about to lose...!

He wouldn't let that happen.

Those words echoed through his mind like a prayer, and that was when he felt something emanate from the Ser Veresta.

"What…?!"

There were no words.

It was a pure, unmediated sense of will.

An emotion close to anger.

Unwillingness. Displeasure. Those were the kinds of emotions it was directing toward him.

What did I do to…?

Though confused, he probed deeper into the Orga Lux's mind.

What was it about him that the Ser Veresta didn't like?

He had always been sincere with the weapon, or so he liked to believe. He had always respected it, and he had always trusted it.

Which was why it should have been willing to help him now.

And yet—

"!"

He had misunderstood.

At that moment, something in his mind clicked.

Right. I've been wrong all this time.

What the Ser Veresta wanted from him—what it wanted from its user—wasn't respect or trust.

More than anything else, *it wanted to be used*, the same as all swords did.

Now that he finally understood that, a voice-like sound echoed through his mind.

That will do.

Then, he felt the Ser Veresta guiding him as his prana harmonized with its urm-manadite core.

"Yaaaaaaaaaargh!"

"Oh…!"

Ayato let out a ferocious roar to precede a slash with the Ser Veresta, cutting straight through the middle of Haruka's blade and forcing her, with a look of surprise, to jump back to safety.

"My, my! Excellent. I knew you could do it, Ayato," she said proudly as she deactivated her blade and returned it to its holder.

"...I have you to thank for that."

In his hands, the Ser Veresta had shrunk to around three feet in length. But it wasn't just the size that Ayato found astonishing—the Orga Lux felt remarkably familiar in his hands now.

By the looks of it, the seal that Haruka had placed over it had also been burned away.

"You're too kind, Ayato. You've been treating Ser Veresta like any other person you might meet, keeping it at a distance. I could see that right away. But you know, that isn't what it wants from you," Haruka said, her gaze a complex mix of affection and severity.

Ayato stared down at the sword in his hand.

"Of course, it won't allow itself to be touched by someone who doesn't give it the proper respect," Haruka continued. "But more than anything, it needs to satisfy its dignity as a weapon. If you're willing to do that for it, it will surely lend you its power."

"If you knew that, why didn't you tell me sooner?" Ayato bit back.

Haruka placed her hands on her hips, lobbing him an amused smile. "What would be the point of that? It wouldn't mean anything if you didn't work it out for yourself."

He had a feeling that was what she would say.

"But I guess you're finally ready now."

"...Huh?"

Just as he was wondering what she meant, Haruka removed her still-functioning Lux from its holder at her waist, the one that she had been using as her secondary weapon until just a few minutes earlier, activating it.

"When I went home, Dad gave me permission to pass them on. He said that you're ready now."

"H-hold on a second. What are you talking about?"

Ayato had no idea what she meant.

"Ayato, I don't think you know this... But there's more to the Amagiri Shinmei style beyond the Hidden Techniques."

"—?!"

Ayato had never heard of any more advanced teachings.

"The Amagiri Shinmei style's Hidden Techniques are designed

to ensure your survival on the battlefield, so they assume you'll be fighting in a melee, right?"

"That's…only natural, seeing as that's how it got started. Isn't it?"

The Amagiri Shinmei style was, after all, developed as a set of techniques to be used by warriors clothed in a full set of armor.

"Indeed. But you know…not all of our fighting forms are inherited from our founder," Haruka explained as she readied her blade. "Ayato, it's time I taught you the Amagiri Shinmei style's Ultimate Techniques."

EPILOGUE

At long last—winter.

“Phew… I don’t think I’ll ever be able to get used to that awful little personality of yours.” Claudia, having awoken before dawn from one of her Pan-Dora-induced nightmares, went to take a shower in an attempt to wash away the lingering chill of her dreams.

Since realizing the truth, her nightmares were becoming more intense. Or to put it more concretely, now even Ayato was among her killers. That said, the situations were so contrived as to be laughable, with the only remarkable thing about them being their sheer vulgarity.

Even so, she wouldn’t allow her dreams to disturb her.

As she let the water wash over her, the nightmare that had gripped her until just a moment earlier became no more than a faint noise, a dull pain fading away to nothing.

“I still need you, so I’ll hold onto you for as long as necessary.” As she dried her hair from her seat on the side of her bed, she murmured softly to herself, as if to put her sense of resolution into words. “But…I wonder whether it isn’t already too late…”

Outside her window, the pale light of dawn began to spill over the eastern horizon.

When the sun reached its zenith, this season's final Festa would be under way.

"Good luck, everyone… Now, especially."

Her efforts over the past months hadn't been in vain.

At the very least, it was probably fair to say she had pinned down Lamina Mortis's identity.

She still didn't have any proof, however.

Besides, if she was right, if it was really *him*, that knowledge would only put Galaxy in an even more difficult position. After all, he was nominally one of their own executives. On top of that, given that he was the executive chairman of the Festa, Galaxy wouldn't be able to take action against him by themselves. The situation would no doubt back her mother even further into a corner.

Their biggest problem, however, was that they still hadn't been able to track down the whereabouts of the Varda-Vaos. Galaxy's highest priority was the recovery or destruction of the Orga Lux; compared with that, Lamina Mortis was little more than a distraction for the foundation. They saw no point in apprehending him if it meant that Varda were to escape.

"At least, that's how Galaxy sees it," Claudia said with a bitter laugh.

In any event, there was a high probability that he would make his move sometime over the next two weeks. Given everything that she had learned about him and his plans, that was obvious enough. The question was when, exactly, he would do it.

He wouldn't want to leave anything to chance.

"…In any event, this year's Lindvolus is going to be a handful. For the contestants and everyone else, as well."

That being the case, she would do what she could to manage affairs on the outside.

As she finished doing up her hair and headed for her dressing room, she nodded to herself with renewed confidence.

*

"Huh…? Is it morning already?" Saya wondered as she made her way through her research and development lab in Seidoukan's harbor block, checking the time only to find that the day really had gotten under way.

Looking toward a corner of the room, she noticed that her assistant, Nueko Kuzukura, still dressed in her white lab coat, had fallen sound asleep. Nueko had been indispensable in the development of the new Luxes. Saya wasn't the kind of person who proactively socialized with others, but outside of the members of Team Enfield, Nueko was probably her closest friend.

"Are you still here?" a voice called as Saya's father, Souichi, suddenly appeared before her.

Or rather, a hologram of him did.

"I can't say that pulling an all-nighter is a particularly efficient use of your resources. To begin with, today's the first day of the Lindvolus."

"I was just making the final adjustments. And besides, I don't have a match today, so it's all right," Saya replied, turning toward an oversized Lux holder positioned in the center of the room. Inside was one of the new Lux models that she had built with her father's and Nueko's help.

"I can't help but be impressed at this young genius I've brought up. I can see now that coming to Seidoukan was the right decision. You've grown, Saya."

"Mm-hmm." Saya glowed, puffing out her chest at the compliment.

"Now you just need to grow a little more on the outside. I'm sure Ayato would love that, too."

"…I'm already growing quickly enough."

"In what way?"

"…My hair, for example."

Indeed, she had grown her hair out considerably over the past months.

"*…Ahhh.*" Souichi let out an exaggerated sigh.

At this response, Saya made to kick him in the shin—but, of course, her foot went straight through the hologram.

As it happened, Nueko had been the one to suggest that she grow out her hair. "You'll knock Ayato off his feet with how cute you are!" she had said. But on top of that, Saya had done it for herself, too.

"I know it's a bit late to ask, but what set your mind on such an exorbitant weapon? And on top of that, you decided to increase the output again, far beyond its original specifications. You shouldn't need anything this powerful just to win the Festa."

"...You're asking that, even knowing that I lost in the semifinals in the Phoenix?"

"Ah...! N-no, I don't mean..."

Saya found herself breaking out into a weak smile as she watched her father fumble for words.

Indeed, her original goal had been to exact revenge on the puppet that had defeated her last time. To that end, she needed a weapon with enough power to break through Ardy's defensive shield with a full-frontal attack.

But the reason she had increased its power beyond that level was to help Ayato.

After all, he had managed to wind up in trouble yet again, this time getting caught in the crosshairs of an incredibly powerful foe.

Ayato and Haruka couldn't defeat this opponent alone. They needed stronger weapons—the more powerful the better.

Ayato's enemy was her enemy. Nor would Saya show mercy to anyone who used Haruka's life as a bargaining chip the way they had.

"Well, I had better go back to my dorm and get ready. I can't go to the Festa looking like this," she said as she fitted the gigantic Lux holder, taller even than she herself was, onto her back.

"*Take care!*" Souichi said with a thumbs-up as he saw her off.

*

Kirin was running alone along the footpath by the lake shore, her sportswear-garbed figure shrouded in fog.

The eastern sky had begun to brighten, although the morning air in the winter was still bitingly cold.

"Haaah… Haaah…"

She moved almost without thinking, her breathing regular and undisturbed. Her silver hair, done up in a ponytail, swept left and right gracefully, fitting the meaning of her first name.

Since meeting Ayato's father, Masatsugu, Kirin had been focusing her efforts exclusively on the most fundamental kinds of training.

Naturally, she had focused on coordinating with her teammates during her training last year in preparation for the Gryps, so in a way, it was good to get back to this kind of strenuous, basic training that could be carried out alone.

Of course, she still engaged in regular practical training matches with Ayato and the others, but she was spending the majority of her days repeating and polishing by herself these most basic techniques.

After all, she knew that the destination that she wanted to reach, the strength that she wanted to obtain, was at the end of this long road.

But as she ran along the lake's edge, she found herself recalling fondly those days before the Phoenix.

I wonder how far I've progressed since then…?

At such times, she always ended up questioning herself like this.

She had gained new techniques and skills, and she had grown both physically and mentally. As a swordswoman, as a person, she had become much stronger than she had been back then.

She understood that.

And yet, there were still so many things in the world that were simply out of her control. She hadn't even been able to be of any help to the person most important to her.

And now the Lindvolus has already started…!

She bit her lip in disappointment but quickly shook her head as she returned to her senses.

Right. There's still time.

Claudia and Helga seemed to be moving forward with a new strategy timed to coincide with the opening ceremony of the tournament.

In that case, all she could do now was polish the edge of her blade.

The edge of the blade that was Kirin Toudou.

But as she once again came to the same conclusion—

"Huh-whaaa...?!"

Trying to veer from the footpath to keep from running into a cat that had appeared in front of her, she found herself stumbling.

She managed to stop herself from falling to her feet, but it took her a little longer than it should have to regain her balance.

The reason for that...was that there was now a little more weight at her chest.

"I didn't need to grow anymore here, though...!"

She had said something similar once and remembered Julis and Saya staring at her in a way they hadn't before or since. And then Claudia had gotten involved, too, and when Ayato had tried to get them to calm down...

Without realizing it, she found herself blushing.

It wasn't just her—they were all thinking about one another.

That was why she knew they would be okay.

*

"...Ah, it got here in one piece."

"Thank goodness! I was worried it wouldn't make it in time!" Flora, on the other side of the air-window, had bloomed into a sweet young lady—but as she clapped her hands together, smiling joyfully, it was clear that she still possessed a childlike innocence.

The parcel that had arrived the previous night rested open atop Julis's lap.

Inside lay a beautiful barrette, shaped like a pair of elegant wings.

"It's a present from everyone at the orphanage! We're all praying that you win! All of the kids and the sisters, His Majesty, too, everyone here in Lieseltania is supporting you! So do your best!"

"...Ah, thanks," Julis replied, averting her gaze as she tried to stop the tears from welling in her eyes.

"Princess...?"

"I'm fine, really. Don't worry about me." Having composed herself, Julis turned back to Flora in the air-window. "I'm grateful for everyone's support. I'll take the crown, I promise you. Just you wait and see."

Julis wondered whether her confident laugh sounded authentic. She wondered, too, just how well she was managing to look like the Julis-Alexia von Riessfeld that everyone thought they knew.

"Of course! I believe in you!" Flora shone her a dazzling, radiant smile.

Julis narrowed her eyes in an attempt to smile back. "Well then," she said, cutting the transmission, and let out a deep sigh.

She slapped herself on the cheeks with both hands as if to wake herself up, before standing in front of the mirror and trying out the hair ornament that Flora and the others had sent her.

What was she supposed to do?

She still hadn't been able to sort things out. Not with Orphelia, not with Ayato, not with Haruka.

With everything still unresolved, a sense of fear never failed to well up inside her at the mere thought of coming to a decision.

But no matter how much she tortured herself, the reality of the situation wouldn't change.

As painful as it was, her deadline for making a decision was fast approaching.

"But until then… I'm going to pull through this. I'm not going to let anything as stupid as fate get in my way…"

No, she wasn't about to give up that easily.

That was what she swore to herself. She finished tying up her hair and reached into the dresser drawer—from which she brought out a handkerchief that she pulled close to her chest.

*

Ayato was waiting outside the main gate leading into Seidoukan Academy as the light of dawn began to break through the morning mist.

"Good morning, Ayato," Haruka called out to him warmly, her faint figure emerging from the fog.

"Morning, Haru."

"Sorry for calling you out here so early. I'm not allowed to enter the school grounds, and I won't be able to go cheer you on today, so I thought...well, I wanted to let you know I'll be with you all the way."

Haruka, now an officer of Stjarnagarm, couldn't have looked more natural in her uniform.

With this year's Lindvolus being the most anticipated in history, the rush of tourists to Asterisk had left every hotel and lodging house completely booked out, and while the tournament had yet to properly get under way, there had already been more trouble throughout the city than at the last Festa. The city guard, already perennially understaffed, had its hands full.

On top of all that, Haruka and Helga were continuing their investigation into Lamina Mortis and his associates.

"Don't worry about it. I'd just finished my morning training anyway."

"Ah... Wait, hold on a second." Haruka suddenly leaned forward, staring intently at his face.

"Huh? Wh-what is it...?"

"Hmm, you should take a bit more care with your appearance. I thought the same thing when I watched the recordings of the Phoenix and the Gryps, actually..."

"R-really...?"

He had to admit he hadn't really put a lot of thought into it.

"At the very least, you can do something with your hair... Come here," she said, before beginning to straighten it up for him.

Ayato found himself suddenly remembering the time when Julis had done something very similar at this very place. It felt like such a long time ago now, but at the same time, it was so close to his heart.

Julis...

Since telling her that he would be entering the tournament, Julis seemed to have distanced herself from him—and from Claudia, Saya, and Kirin, too. Of course, they still said hello whenever they saw each other, but they had hardly ever had lunch or trained together over the past few months.

She had her reasons for doing so—she couldn't give up on winning the tournament.

Just like he couldn't give up on doing everything within his power to keep Haruka safe.

And the fact that she hadn't spoken about it with him no doubt meant it was something that she couldn't discuss.

In that case, he—

"Hey. Don't make such a face," Haruka said, pressing both of her hands against his cheeks as if he were a baby. "That's no way for someone hoping to win a grand slam to look."

"Haruka..." As she patted his cheek warmly, that was all he could bring himself to say.

"It'll be fine."

Ayato looked up. Somehow, those words were enough to lighten his shoulders.

"It'll work out. For you, for me...and for Julis, too."

"...Right. Thank you."

Haruka didn't cast blame for their current situation—not on him, not on herself. She knew just how much it would pain him if she did.

Which was why she kept her parting words simple: "Well, then... You can do it, Ayato."

"I'll do my best." That equally muted response was all he could bring himself to say.

For now, at least.

AFTERWORD

Hi there, Yuu Miyazaki here.

First of all, I'd like to apologize for the delay in getting Volume 12 to you all. I had originally planned to have it ready a little earlier, but I wasn't able to pull it off, and it ended up taking a full year from the release of Volume 11. I'm truly sorry about this.

Also, I mentioned this briefly in the afterword of the second volume of *The Asterisk War: The Wings of Queenvale*, but okiura, our illustrator, hasn't been well this year, and so for a while, we were considering publishing this volume without any illustrations. Nonetheless, after discussing everything with my editors, we decided that okiura's pictures are part of what makes *The Asterisk War* what it is, and they're part of what its fans love about it, too. So even though we ended up making you, the readers, wait a little while, I'm so pleased that we were able to get the work finished with a new set of wonderful illustrations.

Going forward, we've changed the style of the cover illustration to reflect the new story arc. Our protagonists have received new uniforms and hairstyles, and we've gotten our first glimpse of everyone gathered together! Given all the extra challenges involved, and for managing to make our heroines look even cuter and Ayato even cooler, I'd like to doubly express my deepest gratitude to okiura.

Now then, let's touch on what happens this time around (beware spoilers!). If it's fair to say that Volume 11 was mainly about Kirin, then this one is mainly about Haruka. I hope I've been able to bring out her distinctive charm that we've only seen until now in flashbacks and memories. Because depicting her past in detail would probably take another full book, I've only really covered it here in outline form. If I get the chance, I'd love to be able to announce something that deals with this, but seeing as this story is mainly about Ayato and his companions, I didn't want to get too off-topic. On the other hand, seeing as Madiath's and Akari's story directly relates to the main plot of *The Asterisk War*, I wanted to explore it a bit further. The Lindvolus will get under way with the next volume, so expect it to be filled to the brim with battles. Enemies old and new will make an entrance, so I hope you're all looking forward to it as much as I am!

The mobile phone application *The Asterisk War: Brilliant Stella* closed just the other day. I'd like to thank everyone who played it, and all the staff involved in its development.

Last but not least, I'd like to express my gratitude to everyone who helped bring this volume to life.

To O, my editor, to S, who helped edit Fuyuka's Kyoto dialect, to everyone else at the editorial department, to everyone involved in the anime or video game adaptations, and, of course, to all my readers who have supported me on the way, thank you.

I'm looking forward to seeing you all again next time.

Yuu Miyazaki
July 2017

SEIDOUKAN ACADEMY

SOUICHI SASAMIYA

Saya's father. Appears as a holograph after losing most of his body. Technical adviser for Seidoukan's Matériel Department.

SILAS NORMAN

A former companion of Lester's. Attacked Ayato with Allekant's backing but was defeated. Now a member of Seidoukan's intelligence organization Shadowstar.

ALLEKANT ACADÉMIE

SHUUMA SAKON

Student council president of Allekant Académie.

ERNESTA KÜHNE

Creator of Ardy and Rimcy.

CAMILLA PARETO

Ernesta's research partner.

ARDY (AR-D)—"ABSOLUTE REFUSAL" DEFENDED MODEL

Autonomous puppet. Fought alongside Rimcy during the Phoenix.

RIMCY (RM-C)—"RUINOUS MIGHT" CANNON MODEL

Autonomous puppet. Fought alongside Ardy during the Phoenix.

HILDA JANE ROWLANDS

One of the greatest geniuses in Allekant's history. Also known as the Great Scholar, Magnum Opus.

LE WOLFE BLACK INSTITUTE

DIRK EBERWEIN

Student council president of Le Wolfe Black Institute.

KORONA KASHIMARU

Secretary to Le Wolfe's student council president.

ORPHELIA LANDLUFEN

Two-time champion of the Lindvolus and the most powerful Strega in Asterisk.

IRENE URZAIZ

Priscilla's elder sister. Under Dirk's control. Alias the Vampire Princess, Lamilexia.

PRISCILLA URZAIZ

Irene's younger sister. A regenerative.

WERNHER

A member of Grimalkin's Gold Eyes. Kidnapped Flora.

JIE LONG SEVENTH INSTITUTE

XINGLOU FAN

Jie Long's top-ranked fighter and student council president. Alias Immanent Heaven, Ban'yuu Tenra.

XIAOHUI WU

Jie Long's second-ranked fighter and Xinglou Fan's top disciple.

FUYUKA UMENOKOUJI

Jie Long's third-ranked fighter. Alias the Witch of Dharani.

CECILY WONG

Hufeng Zhao's former tag partner, with whom she became a runner-up at the Phoenix.

HUFENG ZHAO

An exceptional martial artist often entrusted with secretarial tasks by Xinglou Fan, who always gives him something to worry about.

SHENYUN LI & SHENHUA LI

Twin brother and sister. Defeated by Ayato and Julis during the Phoenix.

ALEMA SEIYNG

Jie Long Seventh Institute's former number one, with overwhelming ability in martial arts.

SAINT GALLARDWORTH ACADEMY

ERNEST FAIRCLOUGH

Gallardworth's top-ranked fighter and student council president.

LAETITIA BLANCHARD

Gallardworth's second-ranked fighter and student council vice president.

PERCIVAL GARDNER

Gallardworth's fifth-ranked fighter and student council secretary.

LIONEL KARSH

Gallardworth's student council treasurer. A member of Team Lancelot.

KEVIN HOLST

Gallardworth's student council vice president. A member of Team Lancelot.

NOELLE MESSMER

Gallardworth's seventh-ranked fighter. Alias the Witch of Holy Thorns, Perceforêt.

ELLIOT FORSTER

Fought with Doroteo during the Phoenix, with whom he advanced to the semifinals.

QUEENVALE ACADEMY FOR YOUNG LADIES

SYLVIA LYYNEHEYM

Queenvale's top-ranked fighter, student council president, and popular idol.

MILUŠE

Rusalka's leader. Vocalist and lead guitarist.

PÄIVI

Rusalka's drummer.

MONICA

Rusalka's bassist.

TUULIA

Rusalka's rhythm guitarist.

MAHULENA

Rusalka's keyboardist.

YUZUHI RENJOUJI

Studies the Amagiri Shinmei Style Archery Techniques. Acquainted with Ayato.

MINATO WAKAMIYA

Leader of Team Kaguya. Alias Indomitable Perseverance, Kennin Fubatsu.

PETRA KIVILEHTO

Chairwoman of Queenvale Academy for Young Ladies.

VIOLET WEINBERG

Alias the Witch of Demolition, Overliezel.

NEITHNEFER

Queenvale Academy for Young Ladies' second-ranked student. Alias the Goddess of Dance, Hathor.

OTHERS

HARUKA AMAGIRI

Ayato's elder sister. Her whereabouts had been unaccounted for, but she was discovered in a deep sleep, from which Ayato woke her using his wish for winning the Gryps.

SAKURA AMAGIRI (AKARI YACHIGUSA)

Ayato's and Haruka's mother.

MASATSUGU AMAGIRI

Ayato's and Haruka's father.

ISABELLA ENFIELD

Claudia's mother. The top executive of the integrated enterprise foundation Galaxy.

URSULA SVEND

Sylvia's teacher. Her body has been taken over by the Varda-Vaos.

VARDA-VAOS

An Orga Lux capable of usurping the mind of its user. Currently in possession of Ursula's body.

SISTER THERESE

The representative from the orphanage Julis is supporting.

DANILO BERTONI

Former Chairman of the Festa Executive Committee. Died several years ago.

NICOLAS ENFIELD

Claudia's father.

FLORA KLEMM

A young girl from the orphanage Julis is supporting.

HELGA LINDWALL

Head of Stjarnagarm.

MADIATH MESA

Chairman of the Festa Executive Committee.

MICO YANASE

Announcer at the Festa.

BUJINSAI YABUKI

Eishirou's father, and the head of the Yabuki Clan, aka the Night Emit.

JAN KORBEL

Director of the hospital treating Haruka.

JOLBERT

Julis's elder brother and the king of Lieseltania.

LADISLAV BARTOŠIK

A genius researcher in the field of meteoric engineering. Creator of numerous Orga Luxes, including the Varda-Vaos and the Pan-Dora.

RIKKA: THE ACADEMY CITY ON THE WATER

QUEENVALE ACADEMY FOR YOUNG LADIES

Their school crest is the Idol, a nameless goddess of hope. The culture here is bright and showy, and in addition to fighting ability, another criterion for admission is good looks. It is the smallest of the six schools.

COMMERCIAL AREA

MAIN STAGE

CENTRAL DISTRICT

ADMINISTRATIVE AREA

LE WOLFE BLACK INSTITUTE

Their school crest of Crossed Swords signifies military might. They have a tremendously belligerent school culture that actually encourages their students to duel. Owing to this, their relationship with Gallardworth is strained.

SEIDOUKAN ACADEMY

Their school crest is the Red Lotus, the emblem of an indomitable spirit. The school culture values individuality, and rules are fairly relaxed. Traditionally, they have many Stregas and Dantes among the students.

SAINT GALLARDWORTH ACADEMY

Their school crest is the Ring of Light, symbolizing order. Their rigid culture values discipline and loyalty above all else, and in principle, even duels are forbidden. This puts them on poor terms with Le Wolfe.

An academic metropolis, floating atop the North Kanto Mass-Impact Crater Lake. Its overall shape is a regular hexagon, and from each vertex, a school campus protrudes like a bastion. A main avenue runs from each school straight to the center, giving rise to the nickname Asterisk.

This city is the site of the world's largest fighting event, the Festa, and is a major tourist destination.

Although Asterisk is technically a part of Japan, it is governed directly by multiple integrated enterprise foundations and has complete extraterritoriality.

OUTER ...ESIDENTIAL DISTRICT

JIE LONG SEVENTH INSTITUTE

Their school crest is the Yellow Dragon, the mightiest of the four gods, signifying sovereignty. Bureaucracy clashes with a laissez-faire attitude, making the school culture rather chaotic. The largest of the six schools, they incorporate a Far Eastern atmosphere into almost everything.

ALLEKANT ACADÉMIE

Their school crest is the Dark Owl, a symbol of wisdom and the messenger of Minerva. Their guiding principle is absolute meritocracy, and students are divided into research and practical classes. They are unparalleled in meteoric engineering technology.

THE WORLD OF *THE ASTERISK WAR* GLOSSARY

THE INVERTIA

A mysterious disaster that befell Earth in the twentieth century. Meteors fell all over the world for three days and three nights, destroying many cities. As a result, the strength of existing nations declined considerably, and a new form of economic power known as "integrated enterprise foundations" took their place.

A previously unknown element called *mana* was extracted from the meteorites, leading to advances in scientific technology as well as a new type of human with extraordinary powers, called Genestella.

The Invertia was undetected by all the observatories in the world, and the destruction it caused was actually much less than ordinary meteors, so the pervading theory is that it did not consist of normal meteors.

INTEGRATED ENTERPRISE FOUNDATION

A new type of economic entity formed by corporations that merged to overcome the chaotic economic situation following the Invertia. Their power far surpasses that of the diminished nations.

There used to be eight IEFs, but there are currently six: Galaxy, EP (Elliot-Pound), Jie Long, Solnage, Frauenlob, and W&W (Warren & Warren). They vie for advantage over one another and effectively control the world. Each one sponsors an academy in Asterisk.

THE FESTA

A fighting tournament where students compete, held in Asterisk, and operated by the IEFs. Each cycle, or "season," consists of three events: the tag match (Phoenix) in the summer of the first year, the team battle (Gryps) in the fall of the second year, and the individual match (Lindvolus) in the winter of the third year. Victory is achieved by destroying the opponent's school crest, and the rules are set forth in the Stella Carta. As the event is held for entertainment, acts of deliberate cruelty and attacks intended to cause death or injury can be penalized.

The event is the most popular one in the world, with matches broadcast internationally. The IEFs prioritize economic success and growth above all else, so the direction of the Festa has always been driven by the majority demand of consumers. (This is why the fighters are students—viewers want to see beautiful boys and girls fight one another.) Some speak out against the Festa on ethical grounds, but under the rule of the IEFs, those voices have fallen from justified dissent to unpopular opinion.

The cultures of the different schools veer to extremes, which is also by design, for the sake of the Festa.

THE STELLA CARTA

Rules that apply strictly to all the students of Asterisk. Those who violate these rules are harshly penalized, sometimes by expulsion. If a school is found to have been involved, the administration can also be subject to penalty. The Stella Carta has been amended several times in the past. The most important items are as follows:

- Combat between students of Asterisk is permitted only insofar as the intent is to destroy the other's school crest.
- Each student of Asterisk shall be eligible to participate in the Festa between the ages of 13 and 22, a period spanning ten years.
- Each student of Asterisk shall participate in the Festa no more than three times.

MANA

A previously unknown element that was brought to Earth by the Invertia. By now, it can be found all over the world. It responds to the will of living beings who meet certain criteria, incorporating surrounding elements to form objects and create phenomena.

GENESTELLA

A new type of human being, born after regular human children were exposed to mana. With an aura known as *prana*, they possess physical abilities far beyond those of ordinary humans. Genestella who can tap into mana without special equipment are called Stregas (female) and Dantes (male).

Discrimination against Genestella is a pervasive social problem, and many students come to Asterisk to escape this. (The negative bias against Genestella is one reason why opposition to the Festa is in the minority.)

PRANA

A kind of aura unique to Genestella. Stregas and Dantes deplete prana as they use their powers. They lose consciousness if they run out of prana, but it can simply be replenished with time. The manipulation of prana is a basic skill among Genestella, and by focusing it, they can increase offensive or defensive strength. This is especially effective for defense, which explains why serious injuries among Asterisk students are rare despite the common use of weapons.

METEORIC ENGINEERING

A field of science that studies mana and the meteorites from the Invertia. Many mysteries remain pertaining to mana, but experimentation on manadite has advanced significantly. Fueled by the abundance of rare metals found in the meteorites, manadite research has yielded a large variety of practical applications.

MANADITE

A special ore made of crystallized mana. If stress is applied, it can store or retain specific elemental patterns. Before the Invertia, it did not exist on Earth, and it must be extracted from meteorites. Manadite is used in Lux activators, as well as manufactured products developed through meteoric engineering.

LUX

A type of weapon with a manadite core. Records of elemental patterns are stored in pieces of manadite and re-created using activators. By gathering mana from the surroundings, they can create blades or projectiles of light. Mana also acts as the energy source for Lux weapons.

URM-MANADITE

A name for exceptionally pure manadite, much rarer than ordinary manadite. Luxes using urm-manadite are known as Orga Luxes. Urm-manadite crystals come in myriad colors and shapes, and no two are the same. They are said to have minds of their own.

ORGA LUX

A weapon using urm-manadite as its core. Many of them have special powers, but using them takes a toll—a certain "cost." The weapons themselves have something akin to a sentient will, and unsuitable users cannot even touch the weapon. Suitability is measured by means of a compatibility rating.

Most Orga Luxes are owned by the IEFs and are entrusted to the schools of Asterisk for the purpose of lending them to students with high compatibility ratings.